To Fred,
with best wishes,

Kyle

*Nothing
and
Everywhere*

ENJOY THE RIDE!

4/19

4-

Nothing
and
Everywhere

A MORAL TALE

Nigel Lesmoir-Gordon

To order additional copies of this book, contact:
Xlibris Corporation
0-800-644-6988
www.xlibrispublishing.co.uk
Orders@xlibrispublishing.co.uk
302982

Contents

Chapter One   THE ROBBERY 11

Chapter Two   COMB-OVER 16

Chapter Three   CYRIL GOPPIS WUZ HIR 22

Chapter Four   BLACK YACHTING AND
COWBOY JUNKIES 29

Chapter Five   MEETING BIRO 35

Chapter Six   LOST MANUSCRIPTS 41

Chapter Seven   MONEY COMES BY
MYSTERIOUS MEANS 44

Chapter Eight   CYRIL GOPPIS 48

Chapter Nine   CHEROKEE JIM 54

Chapter Ten   SUSIE BELLAVISTA 57

Chapter Eleven   INSTANT KARMA 62

Chapter Twelve   DEAD LINE 65

Chapter Thirteen   OPENING THE HEART 75

Chapter Fourteen   UNITED WE STAND,
DIVIDED WE FALL 77

Chapter Fifteen   DREAM TWISTER 80

Chapter Sixteen   THE TREE OF LIFE 82

Chapter Seventeen   MARCH KLOSSOWSKI........................90

Chapter Eighteen   ROADSIDE ASSISTANCE 96

Chapter Nineteen   THE REGIMENT 101

Chapter Twenty   SNAKES IN THE GRASS..................104

Chapter Twenty One   THE QUEEN OF HEARTS...............110

Chapter Twenty Two   ARE BULLETS PHALLIC?................114

Chapter Twenty Three THE MANDELBROT SET.................117

Chapter Twenty Four   BUSMAN AND A
RIPPLE OF CONFLICT....................121

Chapter Twenty Five   DEAD ANGELS.................................127

Chapter Twenty Six   IT'S JUST A RIDE 138

Chapter Twenty Seven THE AK47 AND THE THREE Ds.....142

Chapter Twenty Eight   EIGHTY 149

Chapter Twenty Nine   THE FIRE IN THE EQUATIONS.....154

Chapter Thirty   FER-DE-LANCE................................156

Chapter Thirty One   THE KNOWLEDGE OF
GOOD AND EVIL.............................159

Chapter Thirty Two   BLOWBACK.......................................161

Chapter Thirty Three   KICK, BOLLOCK AND
SCRAMBLE 166

Chapter Thirty Four   SEMPER FIDELIS 171

Chapter Thirty Five   THE EDGE OF CHAOS 176

Chapter Thirty Six   THE KING AND THE
QUEEN OF SWORDS.......................180

Chapter Thirty Seven   THE DEEP BLUE SEA......................186

Chapter Thirty Eight   EVENT HORIZON 190

Chapter Thirty Nine   SAT CHIT ANAND 197

Chapter Forty   30,000 TANDAR EXIST....................201

Chapter Forty One   SIG SAUER JIGSAW..........................203

Chapter Forty Two   THE LAST STRAW 207

Chapter Forty Three 209

DEDICATION

In memory of:
Raymond Chandler
Benoît Mandelbrot
& Michael Crichton

With special thanks to:
Jenny Lesmoir-Gordon
Lois Kleffman
Kathy Harty
Alastair McNeilage
Samantha Mills
Mike Pitman
Piers Jessop
Damien Enright
Rodney Sims
& Andrew Rawlinson
for their enduring support and encouragement.

God moves in a mysterious way

His wonders to perform . . .

William Cowper 1774

Chapter One

THE ROBBERY

**"'No reason to get excited', the thief he kindly spoke
'There are many here among us who feel that life is
but a joke. But you and I, we've been through that,
and this is not our fate. So let us not talk falsely now,
the hour is getting late'."
Bob Dylan**

North London. Mid-summer 2011. 10:30 am.

"You are nothing and everywhere, John." His guru looked him in the eye.

John was puzzled. "Nothing and everywhere. How can that be?"

"The little you is nothing, John. An illusion. But the big you is everywhere. The consciousness that you are contains everything."

. . . I was rewriting the first chapter of my second novel when I heard a creak on the stairs leading up to the office in

11

my nondescript Edwardian terrace house in a not-very-salubrious part of north London. My mind leapt away from the Jeff Beck song which was running through my head to the front door. I had left it ajar (whoops) to let some paint dry, which I'd been daubing around the chipped edges to smarten the place up. I was trying to sell it. Broke again.

I turned from my screen and was confronted by two men wearing grotesque rock star masks. Mick Jagger and Michael Jackson. Mick was on a giant of a man with legs like tree trunks. He was carrying a gun, which he was pointing at me. I nearly flew through the top of my head. In his wake a skinny little guy, like five matchsticks strung together, swung from side to side as the big one spoke. "Stay calm and don't make any sudden movements, please." He looked me hard in the eye. "We have to lighten your load, Sir, by taking a few essential items off you." His voice was high-pitched and screechy.

"You're going to rob me?"

"That's right, Sir."

"You're going to rob me and you're pointing a gun at me. So why are you calling me 'sir'?"

"Well, Sir, you are the client, are you not?"

"Client!" I gasped.

"Yes, Sir. That's right. As I said, we're going to lighten your load. That's our job."

My mouth was dry, but I managed to croak, "How's that?"

The big man looked around him slowly. The skinny one's head swivelled with him. The big man looked back at me. "You have too much stuff."

"Too much stuff! I've hardly got anything." I licked my lips as I tried to speak with some small degree of confidence.

"You have a computer and a mobile phone I see."

"Most people have those things these days. They're common. Everyone's got these. They're cheap as chips."

"Not to us, they're not,' the skinny one croaked in a very, very deep voice.

The big man turned on him. "Shut up, you. You're nothing."

The little one hung his head.

"That makes you 'everything', I guess," I half-heartedly attempted to joke.

"No, Sir. That's makes me 'everywhere'."

"You're kidding me."

"Why would I kid you, Sir? This is no laughing matter."

"I'm not laughing. But it's pretty spooky."

"Why's that, Sir?"

I was lost for words and scrambled for the right reaction. "You're Nothing and Everywhere! Nothing and Everywhere is the title of the novel I'm writing here—now . . ."

"We thought so, Sir."

"You thought so! What does that mean?"

"It doesn't matter, Sir. Right now we need to relieve you of some, er, items."

"Like what?"

"Your mobile phone, wallet and computer."

"No, please. You can't take my computer. This novel I'm writing is on it." I pointed at the screen.

"Don't you have an external hard drive back up or a laptop?"

"No."

"Well, you should have, Sir."

I felt suddenly indignant. "Look, I can't afford those things. I don't have a car or even a bicycle."

"How do you get about then, Sir?"

"I don't get about. I don't go anywhere. I can't even afford the bus."

"Shopping?"

"What d'you mean 'shopping'?"

"I mean, Sir, how d'you get to the shops?"

"How d'you think?"

"I'm asking you, Sir."

"I walk."

Everywhere moved to my side, glancing at the screen. He put the barrel of the gun to my temple and nudged me. "Your wallet, please, Sir."

I slowly moved my hand to the back pocket of my jeans, gingerly pulled out my old battered wallet and handed it to him. He passed it on to Nothing, who opened it and very carefully went through the contents. He pulled out a fiver and my one charge card, which he passed to Everywhere. The sun came out and splashed across my room through the dirty windows. I could see that Everywhere had very hairy hands. I could also see how filthy and spit-stained my monitor was. I was strangely embarrassed.

"What is the pin number for this card, Sir?"

"Pin number?" I stalled.

"Yes, your pin number."

"I don't know. I can't remember. I hardly ever use it. Just for emergencies."

"How do you pay for things, Sir?"

I shrugged. "Direct debits."

"And where, may I ask, do you get your cash?" His politeness was unnerving.

"Unemployment benefit. I get it weekly at the post office. I pay some into my bank account to feed the service bills—electricity, council tax . . . that kind of thing."

"Give us your pin number, please, Sir."

"It's up there somewhere." I pointed (whoops) at all the post-it notes stuck on the board above my desk.

Everywhere turned to Nothing and squeaked, "Get them down."

Nothing lurched forward as Everywhere stepped back to give him room. The barrel of the gun swivelled round with him, moving to the back of my head. I could feel the hairs on my neck rise up. "No! Please don't take those. My usernames, passwords . . . they're my identity."

"Well, that, Sir, is one of the things we want."

"Why? I thought you wanted my stuff . . . valuables."

"Valuables, Sir?" He squeaked out a nasty, evil chuckle. "You don't have anything of value, do you, Sir?"

"No not really, I guess . . . my phone, my computer."

"Worthless junk," chimed in Nothing. Everywhere glanced at him and he cringed.

"Well, why take them if they're worthless?"

Everywhere shrugged his huge shoulders and sighed, "Well . . . it's our job, Sir, you see."

"No." I was starting to get angry even under the barrel of the gun. "I don't see."

"It's a long story."

"Tell me then."

"It's too long to tell, Sir."

I looked straight into Everywhere's mask. "What's the hurry? I'm not going anywhere."

"No, you're not, but we are." Everywhere leaned into me and I could smell his breath. Surprisingly it was quite pleasant and fragrant. "Unplug that computer. Now," he squeaked.

I clicked the save icon and shut it down, then bent to the back of the machine and started to unplug it. Nothing fidgeted, swaying from side to side.

Everywhere swung round on him and snapped, "Keep the fuck still, you little monster." Nothing nearly left the ground. He hung his head and froze. Everywhere pocketed his gun, picked up my computer and turned to Nothing. "Get his phone and we're out of here."

Nothing darted to my desk and grabbed my phone, stuffing it into his pockets along with my wallet and precious post-it notes. They went back down the stairs and I heard the front door slam as I stared blankly at the empty space in front of me. My book! Gone with the wind. I jumped up and went to the window. Staring through the grime, I scanned the street to left and right. No sign of them. Some shoppers, a couple of hoodies, a drunk. A bus went by and I checked the lower and upper decks. They weren't on it. I turned from the window, ran down the stairs and went right through the ground floor and the back yard to see if they'd dumped the computer on their way out. No sign of it. I stumbled to the front door, opened it and lurched out into the street. What to do? I couldn't call the cops. I had no landline. I hadn't paid the bill and they had cut me off. No mobile now either. Not a penny in my pockets, I started out for the police station. It was a fifteen minute walk and I kept my eyes peeled all the way just in case, but I never caught sight of them.

Chapter Two

COMB-OVER

"Many a true word is spoken in jest."

The local police station was rammed. I took my place in the queue. An hour later I made it to the desk. The duty sergeant looked me up and down. "What can I do for you?" No 'Sir' this time I noted. Funny that.

"I want to report an armed robbery."

"An armed robbery?"

"Yes, by two men," I replied stoically.

"Who was robbed?"

"I was."

The sergeant looked like he didn't believe me. He slid a blank form across the counter. "Name?"

"Danger Smith."

He raised an eyebrow. "Danger Smith?"

I realised my mistake. "No, no," I spluttered. "That's my pen name. My real name is John Smith." I had adopted the first name Danger because my own name was so naff. I mean, who would call their son John if his surname was Smith. It was so unremarkable, so unmemorable. Almost a joke. A joke on me. Danger was a lot cooler and it seemed to work for me. I longed to see it on the cover of a book. It hadn't happened yet. But I lived in hope. Always. Hope springs eternal, doesn't it?

"And where did this armed robbery take place?"

"In my house about an hour ago."

"Was anything taken?"

"Yes." I tried very hard to be patient. "I told you it was a robbery."

"What?"

"What?" I asked back?

"What was stolen?"

"My computer, my wallet, passwords and my mobile phone."

The sergeant scribbled all this down. "And where do you live?"

"16 Archer Street."

"Can you describe the assailant?"

"There were two of them. Look . . . can I please talk to someone about it in . . . er, private?"

The sergeant looked thoughtful for a few moments, then gathered up his notes, turned from the counter and without another word, disappeared through a door at the back of the room. I looked around. I felt completely, as they say, beside myself. It all felt so surreal. I just couldn't focus on what had happened. I waited impatiently for what seemed like another hour. Eventually a side door opened and a middle-aged man in a too-tight suit with combed-over hair came into reception. He looked around him and approached a man in a boiler-suit to my right. I couldn't hear what they were saying, but Boiler-suit shook his head and Comb-over glanced around until his eyes fell on me. He came over, glanced down at his notes and asked, "Mr John Smith?"

"Yes, that's me."

He turned on his heel and muttered, "Follow me, please, Sir."

Ah, Sir again. Unnerving and at the same time reassuring. I followed him through the door and down a long, bland corridor, which smelt of bleach and bodies. He led me into a tiny interview room and pointed to a seat as he sat down in another across a small, grey metal desk.

"So Mr Smith, you say you were robbed at gunpoint and that you live at 16 Archer Street. Is that correct?"

"Yes, that's correct." I could feel myself shaking slightly. There was an air of interrogation about this, which made me uncomfortable.

"You say there were two men. Could you describe them?"

"Er . . . not very easily . . ."

"Why's that, Sir?"

"Well, they were wearing masks?"

"Masks?"

"Yes, masks. Mick Jagger and Michael Jackson."

"So you couldn't see their faces?"

"Obviously not."

"Not obviously, Mr Smith."

Jesus, this man was irritating. "I could definitely not see their faces. I can assure you of that."

"So, what can you say about them . . . any particular . . . ?"

"Yes. One of them was enormous—the one with the gun—really big and with a very high-pitched voice."

"High-pitched voice, Sir?"

"Yes, that's right. A high-pitched voice." I could feel myself getting annoyed. I clenched my hands together under the desk in an effort to hold myself in check and keep my cool. "The other man was small and skinny. And he had a remarkably low voice."

"Strange," mused Comb-over as he noted all this down. He paused then looked up at me. "Anything else?"

"Not that I recall."

"What about the gun, Sir? What type was it?"

"Jesus, I don't know. A handgun. I didn't recognise it."

"Well, was it a revolver or an automatic, Sir?"

"An automatic."

"Was it a real gun?"

"How the hell would I know that? He didn't fire it."

"It might have been a replica."

"Yes, it might. I hear they look very much like the real thing." We were getting nowhere fast. I screwed my hands together harder.

"You told the duty sergeant that they took . . ." He looked down at his notes. " . . . Your computer, wallet, passwords and your mobile phone. Is that right?"

"Nothing has changed in the last hour. So, yes, that's right."

"That's all?"

"Yes." God! This was infuriating.

"No other valuables?"

"No, nothing else. I don't have any valuables. Well, not anymore, that is."

"I can't say a mobile and a computer are valuable . . ."

"Well, the computer was . . ."

"A few hundred quid when new."

"It had my novel on it. The only copy."

"Your novel?"

"Yes, my novel."

"You're a writer, Sir?"

"Obviously." I wanted to strangle him.

"You didn't have any back-up?"

"No." I felt I'd been here before.

"No external hard drive?"

"No. Couldn't afford one. Look, I need you to catch these people. Get my machine back."

"Yes, of course, Mr Smith. That's our job. You didn't happen to catch a name or anything like that, did you?"

"Well, um . . . yes, they did use names." I started to squirm and looked down hard at my feet.

"And?" Comb-over looked hard at me.

"I feel a bit strange saying this, but they did use names. Unusual names. Maybe gangster-type names," I added brightly.

"Which were?"

"Nothing and Everywhere," I blurted out. I felt incredibly stupid as I said it. Comb-over just raised an eyebrow.

"Not very useful that."

"Yes, but maybe they're underworld nicknames. You could surely check on it, couldn't you? Someone here or in your network might know something."

"Yes, someone might and we will certainly check it out, Mr Smith. Now, can you tell me the make of your computer and the serial number?"

I thought hard and tried to visualise the box. But I could not see anything at all in my head. "I can't remember the make and I certainly have no idea of the serial number."

"That's a pity, Sir. What about the phone?"

"What about the phone?"

He sighed. "The make, you know, serial number, model . . . anything you can tell me."

I thought again long and hard. "It was a Samsung, but I don't know the model or serial number. I never took much interest in it. It was just a useful tool for me."

He took a few more notes. "Well, that just about wraps it up for now."

"OK, for you, but I've got no money. I don't get my benefits until Monday."

"What about your bank, Mr Smith?"

"Nothing in it."

"Call your parents or a friend. Maybe someone can help you out."

"But I've got no phone."

"You can make a call from here."

I thought about this. "I don't know any phone numbers. They're all on my mobile phone. I don't bother remembering numbers anymore."

Comb-over sighed. "You're in a bit of a spot then, Sir. I suggest you go to your bank, cancel your card and see if you can borrow something from them."

I nodded dejectedly and got up to leave. Comb-over stood up too, handing me a card. "I'm DS Grimsthorne. Get in touch if you can give us any more information. In the meantime we will see if your description of the men and their . . . er . . . names lead us anywhere, but frankly I doubt it."

I followed him out into the corridor. He paused and turned back to me. "After you've been to your bank what will you do next, Sir?"

I had had an idea, an inspiration as we talked. "I'm going to check all the skips and front gardens in the streets around my house."

"Huh?"

"Well, I figured that once the hoods got out in the light of day they would see that my old computer wasn't worth stealing and was very heavy and they would want to get rid of it in someone's garden or in a skip."

"That's a good idea Mr Smith. Who knows, you might get lucky. Give it a go, OK?"

"I will. I certainly will."

He opened a door for me and I went through reception and out onto the street where I stood shivering in my jeans and t-shirt wondering what the hell to do first.

Chapter Three

CYRIL GOPPIS WUZ HIR

Between a rock and a hard place

I went straight to my bank and, after a considerable amount of waiting and messing around, they were able to stop my card. Surprisingly it had not been used. Unsurprisingly they would not lend me any money.

I got back to my house. It looked depressing and very run-down: peeling paintwork, crumbling walls and dirty windows. I had inherited it from a kindly, if deeply impoverished, aunt. It wasn't in good nick when it fell gracefully into my eager hands. I remain forever grateful to her and hope that one day I meet up with her in heaven to say thanks. As I unlocked the front door, I noticed some scrawly writing over the letterbox. I peered down at it. It was hard to read but it seemed to say: 'Cyril Goppis wuz hir'. Ah, a clue at last. That is if this was written by the robbers and if it was a real name. Here was something I could follow up. I went up to my office. I had a pewter tankard on a shelf where I put my loose change. I emptied it out. Mostly coppers and a few bits of small silver. I counted it up. £2.23. I went down to the public callbox and dialled up DS Grimsthorne. I was connected to his voice mail where I left the briefest possible message, quoting the calling card I had found scrawled on my front door. I said I would call him again in a couple of days since he could not call me.

I caught a bus to Finsbury Park to visit my ex-girlfriend, Amelia. I just hoped she'd be home. As it turned out, she wasn't. I spent the rest of the day sitting hungrily on her doorstep. She came back at 6:30. I was dozing. She gave me a kick. "What do you want?"

"I had an incident today."

"Oh, John, you're always having incidents. Nothing changes."

"I've been robbed. I'm hungry and I've got no money."

"You can come in, but you can't stay. Clear?"

"Got it, Amelia." I stood as she opened the door and I followed her in. She had thrown me out a while back. She had got fed up with my feckless ways and total lack of success as a writer. I followed her into the kitchen. She had a nice flat. Very smart, Spartan in a way. But that seems to be how the affluent like it. Very Feng Shui and very unlike my shambling, rambling, untidy little house.

Amelia was doing well at a flourishing PR agency and was climbing the ladder of power, leaving me very much on the bottom rung. She offered me beans on toast—nothing too ostentatious. I noticed from the can that they weren't the famous brand, but a cheaper supermarket version, which surprised me. Never mind. I was hungry. While I ate I told her about the robbery and my visit to the police station. Amelia looked doubtful.

"Are you making all this up?"

"Why would I do that?"

"Oh, come on, John. I know you and your wily ways of seeking sympathy and getting attention."

"No. I promise you. I know it's very weird, but it's all true."

"Sounds like you might have dreamt it all up to me . . . maybe plunging too deeply into your fantasy novel and getting your lines crossed."

"I swear it's the truth." I think Amelia could finally see that I was genuinely distressed and might be telling the truth. I took the plunge. "I know this will sound daft, but does the name Cyril Goppis mean anything to you?"

"Cyril Goppis! Are you serious?"

"I am. When I got back home after I'd told the cops there was a message scrawled on my front door. It's still there if you want to come and see it."

"No, thanks, John. I'll take your word for it. Just tell me what it said."

"It said: 'Cyril Goppis wuz hir.'"

"That's all?"

"Yup. What d'you think?"

Amelia looked at me and laughed. "I think it's a joke, John. A coincidence or a wind-up. I can't see your robbers bothering or having the time to do that. But . . . I don't know."

She picked up my plate and took it to the sink. "Coffee?"

"Please. I really need that."

She put the kettle on. "What's your next move?"

I thought about this. "Well, somehow I have to find that computer."

"Seriously?

I nodded.

"How?"

"I'm gonna go through all the skips and front gardens in my area and . . . then check the municipal tip. In fact I think I'll do that first."

Amelia stared blankly at me.

"Well, there's no point trying to sell it. It's old. It's not worth anything."

"But it's got your book on it, John."

"OK. And that's why I have to get it back. But it's not worth anything to anyone. I mean, nothing I've ever written has ever been worth diddlysquat and I don't have anything approaching a name in the world of literature."

"I agree. But they might want to rip it off, John."

I laughed for the first time that day. "Thanks for the compliment, Amelia, but they'd have to self-publish! It just wouldn't be worth the effort, would it?"

"I guess not. Is that what you planned to do?"

"Self-publish? Well, I had thought about it . . . if I could afford it. Which reminds me . . . could you lend me 20 quid 'til Monday?"

"God, John. Same old you. But I guess I can." The kettle boiled as she took her wallet out of her bag. It was fairly bulging with notes. She slipped out a 20 and slid it over to me.

"Thanks. I really appreciate it." And I must have looked like I did. She smiled her crooked smile.

"Wanna share a joint with me?"

"No. Thanks. My head's bonged enough as it is."

"Well, I'm gonna have one." She walked to the door, taking her bag with her. "Make your own coffee and let yourself out when you're done . . . and don't take anything with you. Bye."

And she was gone. I poured a cup of coffee and sat down, staring dejectedly at the floor, hardly able to face the task which lay ahead of me. I was depressed, dejected, discouraged, demoralised . . . all of that and more, which was not so strange really when I thought of what I had been through, what had been done to me, what had been stolen from me.

I drank the coffee and muttered, "Bollocks, bollocks, bollocks!" I wondered what I had done to deserve this, pondering. 'As ye sow, so shall ye reap.' I had always felt there was some truth in that, except that the hard, the greedy, the ruthless and the mean seem to be the ones who prosper. Maybe not always, OK, but often. But then you've got to ask what you want out of life. I mean when you're on your deathbed (assuming that's where you die) what are you going to think if you have spent your life screwing people rotten and laying waste all around you, acquiring power and piles of money. As they say, 'you can't take it with you'. I read somewhere that it's best to pop your clogs with a feeling that you have brought something good into the world and spread a little love. I had always wanted my work to earn me a living, of course, but had also hoped—not to be too pompous or arrogant—to throw some light on things like the human condition. I had not been a bad man. I knew that—but I had not always done good things or my very best. I mean, Amelia didn't have a very high opinion of me. That was clear even to my clouded eye. I had never made a relationship work and I was staring 35 in the face. I wondered if I was just too self-centred and should have done more to put others first.

Anyway, enough of that kind of reflection. I had to get on with the narrower task at hand. I finished my coffee, put the mug in the sink, left the kitchen and tried to let myself quietly out of the front door. Annoyingly it slammed loudly behind me. I looked up as Amelia pulled a curtain aside. She looked down on me. I waved. She did not wave back. I shrugged, but did not really feel that casual. In fact I felt even more dejected and wondered again—for the thousandth time—why she didn't like me.

I slunk off down the street in a distracted kind of way and I'd gone over half a mile before I realised I was going in the totally wrong direction. About turn. As I passed Amelia's house I saw a brand-new silver Porsche draw up. I stopped and watched as a sharp-dressed, good-looking guy got out and skipped nimbly up to her front door. I turned away more disgruntled than ever and pounded away up the street.

The tip was open for business. As I went in I noticed a sign that said that nothing could be removed from the site, which made me paranoid and a bit uneasy. I sidled over to the container for small electrical devices, looking around somewhat nervously. I saw many hair driers, razors, printers and quite a few desktop computers. I wondered briefly if the people who dumped their computers here had wiped them clean or removed their hard drives. Not my problem though, I thought. I clambered into the container and started rummaging through the machines. After a few minutes I concluded that my PC was not there. I would have at least recognised its colour and the on-off switch. I left the site, whistling in a relaxed, off-handed kind of way, which was all in vain because nobody paid me any attention.

Where next? Back to the house and a street-by-street search of skips and front gardens. I was beginning to feel hungry again, but knew I had to ignore the gnawing if I was to survive until I could collect my benefits. 20 quid wouldn't go far.

After a long chaotic search I found my map of the local area and set about marking off squares with a semi-dry red pen. I had a plan and I was pleased with myself. It looked like rain so I decided to get started. I turned right outside my door and headed north. Taking the first turning on the left I strolled along looking as casually as I could into every front garden. I could see a skip up ahead of me on the same side of the road. My pulse started to race and my mouth went dry as I got closer.

I started to nose around in the skip. I heard a window slide open with a clunk.

"What the fuck you doing?"

I looked up. A bull-necked skinhead was looking down on me. I shrunk back. "I . . . I'm looking for my computer."

"Whatcha mean?"

"My computer has been stolen and I wondered if it might have been chucked in here." I nodded at the skip.

"Why the fuck would it be in there?" Skinhead was clearly getting more and more angry.

"Well, I live just round the corner and I thought the thieves might have just thrown it in here."

"Why would they do that?"

"I dunno. Maybe it was getting heavy or they realised it wasn't worth anything once they saw in the daylight how old it was or . . ."

"Shut up and fuck off or I'm coming down there!"

"OK, OK. I'm on my way. Sorry." I scuttled off as fast as I could without actually running. Didn't want to look too intimidated or uncool. In fact I was very intimidated and was feeling decidedly uncool. I'd never been big on physical courage and standing up for myself.

I approached the next skip in the next street with greater caution while I pondered whether this kind of search might be easier as a late-night op. Even though the sun was setting it wasn't dark. I thought about the lighting issue and concluded that a torch would not be a good thing and that I would need the skips to be under or near a street lamp. This was not turning out to be as easy as I thought and I was getting hungry. I did another two skips then abandoned the search while I nipped down to the supermarket to pick up some cheap and cheerful provisions. I remembered seeing a doc on TV about people who fed themselves out of supermarket bins with food that had passed its sell-by date. This, I thought, would kill two birds with one stone. I could check the shop's skips for my computer while I collected my supper. I felt a little cheered up by this minor brainwave. A bit of a bounce came back into my step.

Chapter Four

BLACK YACHTING AND COWBOY JUNKIES

**Some people tap their feet. Some people snap their
fingers. Some people sway back and forth. I just sorta
do 'em all together."
Elvis Presley 1956**

*A brief clip from the screenplay for the proposed film I wrote called THE
MYSTERIOUS MICHAEL A:*

Margaret enters. She carries a plate of sandwiches which she
sets down beside the laptop. She sneaks a look at the screen.
Michael is aware of her trying to read.

MICHAEL
It's my work.

MARGARET
Oh, is it? I'm sorry. I really
didn't mean to be nosey.

MICHAEL
It's all right.

MARGARET
I always wanted to write myself.
I thought I had a novel in me,
but I never knew how to get started.

MICHAEL
Well, you're right. It's the
starting that's the hardest thing.

MARGARET
Really?

MICHAEL
Oh, yes.
(Michael turns to her)
You know, I am sure you *do* have a novel in you.

MARGARET
Oh, do you think so.

MICHAEL
Oh, yes.

MARGARET
How can you tell?

MICHAEL
Well, everybody has a novel in them.

MARGARET
Oh . . . do they?

Margaret is crestfallen. She is lost for words.

Next day after much fretting and fuming I went out for a
stroll and as I walked my mind went scurrying back to the year

I had spent in LA trying to sell a screenplay I had written called '*The Mysterious Michael A*'. I couldn't get anyone interested most probably because I didn't know anyone. Anyone in power, that is. I knew a few people, of course, but they were nearly all like me, struggling to get a foot in the door. The two not-very-successful producers I had persuaded to look at my script said it was too obscure, which is odd because it was a simple story about life and money. They told me I needed to get a named director or some acting talent on board to put together a whole package. This was totally beyond me and my very limited funds.

I had made friends with another English guy called Oscar, who had moved to California two years before me and was trying to make it in the porn movie industry—on the production side that is, not in front of the camera. Unbelievably he couldn't break into this world either. Oscar and I partnered up as painters and decorators. We had been commissioned to do a very difficult job. We were running late and the traffic was fubar. My cell phone battery was flat and Oscar had forgotten his. I was pretty strung-out. Our client was a stickler for promptness and we still had some supplies to pick up. It was going to be a difficult and explosive morning.

Oscar beat his hands on the steering wheel. "This is fucked, John. There are just too many damned cars."

"At the risk of stating the obvious, Os. But, yes, you're right. Amazes me they still continue to design 'em, make 'em, push 'em and sell 'em."

"Carmageddon. Whatever you call it. Fact is we just gotta sit here and crawl like snails."

And we did. I was abruptly aware that Oscar had started speaking in American. His voice had taken on a new twang and whine. Maybe I should listen to myself.

"Talking of cars, Oscar, have you heard the one about the parrot and the car salesman?"

"Nope."

I launched into the joke with much forced enthusiasm and Oscar cracked up as I knew he would. That kind of a joke appealed to him, if not so much to me. I never did go in for the coarse style gags. They never did it for me. Still don't. I like jokes neat and witty and I like telling them. I believe I have a good delivery and get the pacing right, putting out a nicely pitched punch line. And you could say that, although I was just about at my wits end, I had not lost my sense of humour. But, I noted, I had indeed taken on an affected American accent.

Oscar tapped his hands on the steering wheel. It was hot in the car even with the windows down. The a/c was shot and we didn't have the wedge to cover it. "You gonna watch the game tonight?"

"Nah. Not interested."

"Don'tcha like football, John?"

"Football?"

"Yeah, football."

"Oh, come on, Oscar. You know I can't stand football. Sport sucks."

"All sport?"

"All sport. Complete waste of time. 22 grown men running up and down a patch of green throwing and kicking a ball to get it over a line or something just doesn't do it for me. Monkeys could do that."

"What about motor racing? Surely you like that."

"Jesus, no, Oscar. I call that black yachting."

"Black yachting?"

"Yeah. Like grown men and women hurling themselves round a track in little metal boxes risking life and limb. It's ridiculous. Boring, waste of money and very, very dangerous. That's why I call it black yachting."

Oscar looked puzzled so I added, "Elvis' yachting cap was black. How cool is that?"

Oscar laughed.

"It's true. I've seen a picture of him wearing it."

"No shit, John. But, I guess it's the kinda thing the king of rock would wear."

The car inched forward through the thickening smog.

"You know, Oscar, the other thing I don't get off on is that sport is all about winning. Competition. I don't like it. I can't believe that evolution—whatever—is about survival of the fittest. I think it's about cooperation. Symbiosis. Harmony. That kind of thing."

"And what the fuck is symbiosis, John?"

"It's like when one organism depends for its existence on another and vice versa."

My mind wandered like a loose cannon. "Cowboys don't do sport."

"Beg your pardon, John?"

"Cowboys don't do sport."

"Yes, they do, John."

"How so?"

"Rodeos."

"Is that a sport, Oscar? I don't think so."

"Course it is."

"Never seen it like that. Thought it was more like . . ."

"It's sport, John."

"Well . . . I guess."

"It's physical. It's competitive. In my book that's what makes it a sport."

"OK, Oscar. You win I lose."

Our conversation rambled on, loosely focused on cars and transport. We speculated on an oil-free world and the political implications with energy coming from other, cheaper sources. We could see that the creaking power bases would shift and change. New dynasties would emerge, maybe whole new political systems—not capitalism, not communism: something else entirely, which we could not then even imagine.

Oscar and I were a couple of losers in LA. I didn't make it with my screenplay and neither of us ever found a girlfriend either and not for want of trying. Not too surprising I guess. Our car was a wreck and our apartment wasn't exactly salubrious. You would never want to take a girl back there. I was a lot tidier and cleaner than Oscar, but it was a losing battle. Our apartment was a perfect example of the principle of entropy in the universe: that the whole thing is steadily rolling into disorder. If things are left to themselves they will just get more and more disordered. Dust to dust. You have only to witness little children or a puppy and how they can turn a house upside down in 10 to 15 minutes. Fallen trees crumble, break up and return into the soil. Wrecked cars left over decades eventually collapse into heaps of rust. Dead bodies go quickly into entropy. Decay sets in fast.

And even the sun's burning out and heading for collapse. Of course that's far, far in the future. But, I guess, it means that all stars will eventually burn out. And that's got to mean that the universe is heading towards 'lights out' and absolute blackness. I know it's not my problem, but it bears thinking about, doesn't it—in terms of what it all means, or doesn't mean? Was there a beginning and is there to be an end? Is that utter darkness the end? Or does it start over again as is proposed in a variety of mystic texts. You've got to wonder.

I am not convinced by the Big Bang theory. Just a gut feeling, of course, because I am not a physicist or astro-physicist working at the leading edge of origin research. I take the view that you don't necessarily need a bang to get a universe going. Matter might have slowly appeared throughout space, which might have come with it, condensed out of a slowing down of the vibration of the master wave to become particles. This is what Fred Hoyle proposed in his Steady State theory. And then there's the de Sitter model too, but I don't know anything at all about that.

Chapter Five

MEETING BIRO

László József Bíró 1899-1985
The inventor of the ball-point pen

I went into my local park and found a bench in the sunset. There was a nice warm glow and I started to relax in the golden balm. I took a nap and had a peculiar dream. I was wearing greasy jeans and a filthy white t-shirt, working as a roadie for the Rolling Stones. I knew I was working for the Stones because I could see Mick and Keith having a heated argument off to the side of the enormous stage. I was running out cables, placing amps and speakers along with a group of other men who were doing their best to ignore the two rock stars. A film crew were setting up cameras in a half-hearted kind of way. A man, who I took to be the director, was poncing around in skin-tight jeans and smoking a fag in a long cigarette holder. He was pointing this way and that, making that silly screen shape with his fingers and peering through it every now and then at the stage. He oiled his way over to me as Mick broke away from Keith with a shrug and came in my direction. Both men reached me at about the same time. Mick nodded to the director figure. "This is the one."

The director bowed in an obsequious kind of way and turned to me. "We are ready to do the interview now."

"What interview?"

Mick scowled at the director and whined in the way he does, "Didn't you tell him?"

The director squirmed. "I . . . thought my P.A. had." He turned to me. "Didn't Doris tell you?"

"Tell me what?"

"'Bout the interview?"

"I don't know what you're talking about."

I woke with a jerk as two squealing kids started scrambling over the bench. I was very hungry and not much refreshed. I got up and walked away. I was in a bit of a daze and was nearly knocked down by a silent cyclist, who cursed as she swerved around me. "Don't you have a bell?" I barked. She turned, nearly taking out an elderly stroller, and gave me the finger, "Charming!" I thought as I continued on my way. The dream came back and I pondered its meaning. There was a Mick connection with Everywhere obviously, but the meaning of the interview thing eluded me. I shrugged and headed for the supermarket with an empty shopping bag I'd picked up in the park. The sun was setting and I had to work fast.

I slunk quietly into the yard behind the store and started work. Luckily there was no one around, but I worked fast in any case. The skips were easy to access using the battered steps I found by the gates. The first skip was loaded with pre-packed fruit and vegetables, which was fine by me—I'm a vegetarian. I found spinach, onions, potatoes, broccoli, strawberries, raspberries, bananas and some brown bread. But no computer. I didn't want to look any further so I climbed down quickly, returned the steps and scooted out through the yard gates as two people came out of the shop's back door for a fag break. I walked home through the golden evening. I passed an off-license, thought briefly of vodka, but moved on by. I'd had a serious run-in with booze in years gone by. It had been hard to kick the habit and I didn't want to go there again. Funny thing is that booze is so cheap when it's such a short-lived pleasure with a heavy price.

I got back to my house and made supper. During my bachelorhood I had become quite a nifty cook and mostly ate well. I took my supper up to my office, catching sight of the sad and empty, dust-free rectangle on my desk where my computer had been. It was a painful, stomach-fluttering moment, which left me in a world of hurt and feeling demoralised. I had a horrible sense of loss—like mourning the death of an old friend. I had to get it back. I couldn't live without it—the novel, that is. Not the machine itself. Like the thieves had said, that was junk. There had been other occasions when I had written a page or two and the machine had crashed or there had been a power cut and I had lost my most recent work and I had gone spare—a complete freak-out—feeling for all-the-world as if I had lost a loved one. Trying to rewrite the crashed stuff was an unspeakable horror. I would never get it back in its original, finest and pristine form, which was total bollocks of course. But this time it was different. Losing the entire work I considered that I was justifiably desperate and depressed.

Question was, though, how the fuck to get it back? Talk about needles in haystacks! I ate my supper in an extremely low mood, wracking my brains for a way to track it down. Hopeless really. Apart from checking front gardens and skips I had no other ideas.

Then my luck broke and in a most unexpected way. Out of the blue I met Biro.

Next morning when I was discreetly doing another skip and I had my head buried in the junk I heard some scratching over on the opposite side. I looked up and out of the corner of my eye I saw the head and shoulders of a well-built guy with cropped hair. I guessed he was a few years older than me. He looked at me and winked. I was momentarily thrown.

"Hi," he said in a very friendly kind of way. No threat there.

"Hi," I replied with enthusiasm.

"Find anything?" he asked.

"Nah."

"What you looking for?"

"Nothing special." He peered at me over the top of the skip. I peered back. "What about you?"

"Furniture."

"Really?"

He shrugged. "Yup. Small stuff obviously."

"Obviously"

"Well, I can't shift anything big, can I?"

"No, I guess not. No car?" I asked.

"Well, hardly . . ." He looked back into the skip and rootled around for a bit then resurfaced. "Nothing here."

"Doesn't seem to be."

"Biro's the name. Hungarian. Means 'judge' Wanna meet for a drink later?"

"Yes, sure. Thanks." I walked round the skip and offered my hand. "I'm John." He shook my hand with great vigour and enthusiasm. I took a liking to him. "Where and when?"

He thought hard for a moment, looking at the sky. "The Castle. 6 o'clock."

We parted company and I went for a stroll. It was a fine evening. I got myself down to the canal and saw some unpleasant looking young men there. I pretended I didn't see them and scarpered in a nonchalant kind of way.

The Castle was a run-down shambles, badly in need of renovation. My guess was that it wasn't in line for any investment and that most likely they were just letting it go until the brewery shut it down. When I arrived there the bar was virtually deserted. Biro was already sitting at a table by the window. I couldn't miss him. In the setting sun he looked astonishing. Mostly because he was wearing a bright, apple green suit. I walked over to him. "Hi."

"Hello, John. Have a seat. What would you like?"

"Alcohol free lager, please, Biro." He raised a sinuous eyebrow and walked over to the bar. He moved well with a kind of John Wayne roll. He intrigued me.

We chatted about this and that for an hour or so. I asked him if he was related to László Bíró, the inventor of the ball point pen.

"No. Sadly not," he responded, "but my father was a fan of his and gave me the name. Biro was a clever man. He made quite an impact."

I suddenly found myself blurting out, "D'you know anyone called Cyril Goppis?"

He looked hard at me and didn't respond immediately. He took a drink. "Why?"

I gave him a compressed version of the robbery. He listened intently. I finished. He was silent for a while. I waited.

"Yeah, I know Cyril."

I was gob-smacked. "You do!" I could hardly believe it. What a coincidence. "Who is he?"

"Small-time hood with Russian mafia connections."

"You're kidding."

"No, I'm not, John."

"He's not one of those guys who stole my stuff is he?"

"No. Your descriptions don't fit with Cyril."

"How d'you know him, Biro?"

"Let's just say our paths crossed once a year ago. I was visiting my family in Hungary and I met him there. He's not someone I would want to be around long or get to know well."

I flashed on something I'd read recently. The theory of six degrees of separation: everyone is on average approximately six steps away from every other person on Earth. So, on average we can connect with any two people in six steps or fewer, which threw some light on this connection. I came back with a question, "What's Goppis do?"

"He's a gangsters' gopher. Running small-time numbers for big-time operators."

"So who would have put his name on my door . . . and why?"

"No idea, John."

"Really? No idea?"

"Well, I guess someone is trying to help you."

I stared out of the pub window at the slow-crawling traffic. Turning back to Biro, I asked, "Isn't that a bit strange . . . giving me a lead? I mean, who would do that?"

"Maybe it was Cyril Goppis."

"D'you think?"

"Well, Johnny boy, it's the obvious place to start."

"So, how do I find him?"

"Not easily. But I can ask around. Meet me back here tomorrow. Same time. And I'll see what I got. OK?"

"Great, Biro. Thanks a lot."

"In the meantime I would finish checking the skips if I were you."

"Will do."

He got up and was out of the pub before I could even say goodbye. I stayed there for a bit, staring at the balding, filthy carpet and contemplating this turn of events.

Chapter Six

LOST MANUSCRIPTS

"Why is there something rather than nothing?"
M. Michell Waldrop

My mind slipped sideways into another fuzzy memory, which sharpened up somewhat as I pondered it. I recalled that in 1919 T E Lawrence (of Arabia fame) completed a draft of his book Seven Pillars of Wisdom. On his way to deliver the manuscript to his publishers, making a change at Reading Station, he left his briefcase on the train. He had copies of the introduction and the last two chapters, but all the rest—250,000 words—was gone! Early the next year he started the utterly daunting task of rewriting as much as he could remember of the first version. The poor man had destroyed his wartime notes and had to rely on his memory. He thought the rewrite was hopelessly bad. Yikes! This really depressed me.

The thought of having to start my book again overwhelmed me. As I've said, I didn't see how I could get them back again just as they were in all their original pristine, elegant perfection. I felt like chucking myself in the river. I ran from the pub and down to the chip shop.

On the way I passed a stationer's. I love stationery shops. They are my favourite along with bookshops, of course. I love the smell of paper and the look of empty clip files, envelopes, notebooks and racks and racks of pens. There is so much potential there: blank pages, files to be filled and ink to be used up. They give me optimism and present me with a bright and glowing future of success, money, fame, admiration and respect. I stopped to savour the view and caught sight of myself in the window, wondering for a moment, just who this tired, dejected-looking man could possibly be. Was it me? It couldn't be, but it was. I considered that I wasn't bad looking. I was tall, athletic and with some muscle on me. I had 'interesting' grey eyes, a good nose and, they tell me, a strong mouth. I certainly had a good head of hair—thick, brown and a bit wavy. I had always felt comfortable with my looks, which was helpful. I resolved there and then to wash my hair, shave and change my clothes

I sat on a bench feeling lost and lonely, munching through my supper. I had to keep a grip and fight off the ghastly black cloud, which threatened to engulf me, and get my act together. A tired looking drunk was stumbling along the pavement. He tripped and fell flat on his face. He put out his hands to break his fall and one of them went straight into a splat of dog shit. I heard him groan and watched him attempt to clean his hand on a page of dirty newspaper. *The Daily Mail* to boot. Ironic. At first I made no effort to help him and perhaps even relished his misfortune with a discreet *schadenfreude* moment. It made me feel better for a couple of seconds and then horribly guilty. But then I found myself walking over to help him to his feet. I couldn't help it. He mumbled some incomprehensible thanks and wobbled off on his way to god knows where. I felt a momentary glimmer of self-satisfaction with my good deed, but the glow soon faded and I was back in my own very personal and uncomfortable gloom space.

Although I felt bloated with food and gloom I eventually pulled myself together and went off in search of skips, little expecting what would happen next. In fact I could never have guessed it in a thousand years. It was the equaliser. A dream come true. I started off two streets from my front door. The first skip I came across was half empty and I could tell at a glance that my computer was not in it. I moved on. Nothing in the next street then, rounding a corner, I spotted a recently burnt down house with two big skips outside. I remembered this event: the fire engines howling, the smoke, the sealed-off roads and the chaos. It was mildly exciting at the time, watching from the safe vantage point of my office window.

As I stealthily approached my quarry I remembered being told the story of the New Yorker, who realised when the results were posted that he had entered the winning numbers for a big lottery. He couldn't find his ticket though and concluded that he must have put it out with his rubbish. He spent the next few weeks churning through the city's garbage tips, but to no avail of course. I wasn't convinced of the truth of this tale. Maybe it was just made up but it was another dispiriting memory, which did absolutely nothing to lift my spirits off the ground where they were painfully scraping along between my legs.

Chapter Seven

MONEY COMES BY MYSTERIOUS MEANS

**"Why isn't the universe just a turbulent mess of
particles tumbling around each other? Why are there
structure, form and pattern?
Why is consciousness possible at all?"
Martin Heidegger, philosopher**

I approached the first skip outside the burnt house with some
caution and with 'more advised watch'. I peered into its depths.
In the blackness I saw something shining. I reached in, scraping
the skin of my ribcage in the process and felt around. My fingers
caught on a handle. I got a grip and lifted. Out came a briefcase.
I did a cursory and cautious examination, thinking the while
about booby-traps and bombs. Turning it round into the light
I saw the initials JS embossed in gold on the front. Bit spooky.
My initials. Well, I thought, this is mine and it's going home with
me.

I felt self-conscious in my jeans and t-shirt with the shiny
black briefcase, but I swung along as nonchalantly as I could. In
any event no one took any notice of me.

I slipped in through my scarred front door and took the
case up to my office. I put it on my desk and studied it with
some suspicion. To open or not to open, that was the question.
A bomb or not a bomb. I knew from carrying it home that it
was not empty. Something was banging around inside. I took a
deep breath and, with sweating palms, I opened the two clasps.
I was still there. I walked over to the window in an attempt
to calm down. I stood there, staring vacantly into space and
hyperventilating. I walked carefully back to my desk. My hands
were slick with sweat. I took the bull by the horns and flicked the
lid open. I jumped back, covering my face with my hands as one
does. Then peeping through my fingers, the most extraordinary
sight greeted my eyes. The case was full of money: stacked and
wrapped bundles of 50s. I was gob-smacked. Still thinking there
might be a booby trap, I very cautiously picked up a stack and
thumbed through it. Solid money. I could see at a glance that
there must've been around £200,000 there at least. Sticking out
in the bottom left-hand corner was what looked like the muzzle
of a handgun. I moved some money aside and there it was: an
automatic. I could read the name Sig-Sauer p226 9mm on the
barrel. I pulled it out of the case and weighed it in my hands. It
felt heavy and real. I put it on my desk and lifted out the money.
There were two magazines in the bottom of the case. I could see
they were full of shiny brass and copper bullets with snub noses.

I had to sit down. I needed a cup of tea. I stared at the money.
I waited a few minutes for my knees to stop shaking then went
down to the kitchen and put the kettle on. While it was boiling I
went to my front door and double-locked it, pulling through the
safety chain. I double-locked my back door too. I poured water in
a cup and waited for the tea to brew. My head was spinning. I felt
suddenly empowered and full of potential, but couldn't avoid
considering the ethical position. Should I hand the money in
and, more importantly, should I hand in the Sig-Sauer? I quickly
and rather surprisingly concluded that the answer to both
questions was 'No'. Although it wasn't hard convincing myself,
I experienced a moment of guilt as I wondered what my guru
would think of this.

I took my tea upstairs and started considering hiding places. I
decided on a floorboard. I drank my tea then went back downstairs

to collect some tools. Back in my office again I rolled up the tired rug and set about loosening a board. It wasn't easy, but I did it without too many signs of a struggle. I put the automatic, the magazines and most of the money in the cavity under the floorboard, holding back two bundles of notes. I replaced the board, fixed it down and rolled the rug back into place. I walked over the board over a few times and it didn't squeak and it wasn't loose. Ideal. I recalled those immortal lines of John Lennon on The White Album:

'When I hold you in my arms
And when I feel my finger on your trigger
I know nobody can do me no harm.
Happiness is a warm gun, momma.'

. . . and I took some comfort from them even though there's considerable irony there when you stop and consider what fate befell Lennon at the end of the barrel of Mark Chapman's gun. But I put that negative thought right out of my mind immediately.

I slept well that night and next morning I left the house and walked down to the mini-cab company. I told them I needed a car to take me round central London for a few hours and fixed a rate. Within minutes I was on my way to Bond Street. When we arrived at the top of the street I asked the driver, who was called Ishmael, to drive slowly along while I looked out for a men's tailor shop. I spotted Aspley, Boilerman & Guise and asked Ishmael to pull over and drop me off. I took a card with his mobile number and suggested he cruise around or park while I did my shopping.

The shop was very upmarket, but scruffy as I was, I strolled right in. I was confident. I had money. To cut a long story short they were very polite and I bought two black Ravello single-breasted suits, one dark grey Armani double-breasted and six silk shirts of various colours, mostly black. They were happy with the cash so I grabbed my bag and was on my way. Three doors down I caught sight of a shoe shop I liked the look of aptly called Emil Proudfoot. I bought two pairs of beautiful black hand-made leather shoes.

Next I needed a new mobile. I phoned Ishmael from the shop's phone and told him where I was. He picked me up within a couple of minutes and I asked him to find a phone store. He opened his own phone and googled. He drove me to the T5 Network shop in Oxford Street and dropped me off.

I asked an assistant for the top of the range smart-phone. They recommended a PRC Necromancer 43. I said that would be fine by me and we did the paperwork. It didn't take long. I called Ishmael again and said I was ready to head for the nearest Apple store. By the time he picked me up he knew where to go and we were on our way. I bought an iPad2 and set it up.

I was feeling vigorous and optimistic when I arrived home. I set up the Mac, played around a bit and went online. Nothing much in the way of emails, only the usual Viagra stuff and you have $23 million waiting to collect if you would let us have your details . . . blah, blah. My circle of friends seemed to be forever shrinking. I sent an email to an agent, who had not yet turned me down, to ask if she had read any more of my first novel and one to my mother to assure her I was OK and doing nicely. I didn't mention the robbery, of course. It wouldn't have done either of us any good to have shared that.

I googled Sig-Sauer P226 and found the operating manual, glanced at it and closed it down. Just so I knew it was there. I like to be thorough sometimes.

Chapter Eight

CYRIL GOPPIS

The boondoggle kicks off.

I was in The Castle at 6:00 to meet Biro, looking cool in my Armani suit and black shirt. I bought him a drink when he arrived. We sat in a dirty, dark and quiet corner.

"You're looking good, John."

"Yeah, well I thought I should smarten myself up for the business in hand. How'd it go?"

"I got it for you."

"Great, Biro. Well done."

"Goppis has a place up in Finchley." He handed me a card. "My number's on there too. What you gonna do, John?"

"Go and see him and find out who he works for."

"Won't tell you that."

"He will, I think. I'm very persuasive and I have some leverage."

"You're gonna need it, John . . . D'you want me to come with you?"

"No, thanks, Biro. Not for this, but I may well need your help later."

"OK, OK. Just let me know. I'd like to help you. Wanna know what's going on."

I took a cab up to the rough end of Finchley and asked the driver to wait. The front door of the block was open and falling off its hinges. I walked up to the piss-stink second floor and pressed the bell of Goppis' door. It didn't work. I knocked and soon heard a shuffling inside and then a muffled voice. "Who's there?"

"Friend of Biro's. Said we might do some business together." I spoke calmly and gently, being as friendly as I could.

"You alone?"

"Sure."

The door opened a crack and a skinny grey face peered out at me. I smiled broadly. "Hi, Cyril."

He opened the door and let me in. The flat was very basic, sparely furnished, filthy and badly in need of decoration. It was as much as I had expected. He looked me up and down and seemed satisfied that I wasn't a threat.

I had seen enough hard-core cop movies and mafia tales to play the part I was taking on. I felt like steel and held on to that. He led me into his sitting room and pointed to a seat. I sat on a wobbly, half broken chair.

"So, what can I do for you . . . uh . . . ?"

"John. John Smith."

"So, what can I do for you . . . John?"

"It is my name. My real name. Uninspiring as it is, that's it, Cyril."

He stared at me, waiting. I let him sweat it a bit.

"Who do you work for, Cyril?"

"What?"

"Who do you work for?"

He flinched like I had touched a sore. "None of your business."

"Yes, it is, Cyril."

"Why?"

"Because, Cyril."

"Because what?"

"Because I want to know."

"You'll have to wait 'til hell freezes over, John, before I tell you that."

"No, I won't, Cyril."

He attempted to stare me out, but I was resolute. I pulled the Sig-Sauer out of my jacket pocket very smoothly and aimed at him. "Speak up, Mr Goppis. The ball is now, as you can see, very definitely in your court."

He still did not answer my question. Looking at me over the barrel of the gun, he shivered and I said, "You will tell me. This weapon takes sugar gliders. Do you know what one of those will do to you?"

"I know what sugar gliders are."

I did too. I'd read about them somewhere, but didn't really know what kind of bullets I had. It made me sound tough so I stuck with it.

"Well you know then, you little fuck, that one shot will make a hole in you big enough to push a football through and a large part of you will end up on that wall." I looked over his shoulder. "So, speak. I'm running out of patience." I slid back the bolt with my left hand with a nice solid clunk, chambering a round. I saw him flinch and his courage drain somewhat. I flicked off the safety with a flourish. He looked at my trigger finger and sighed.

"Who do you work for, Goppis?"

"I just can't tell you that."

"Why not?"

"They'd kill me if they found out."

"Would they now, Cyril? Well, let me put it to you like this: if you don't tell me now—right now—I will kill you. So, taking your chances, you have longer to live if you play ball with me." I thought momentarily about my guru and what he would have to say about my lying and heavy-handed tactics. I flinched this time but put the thought out of my mind and soldiered on. "You should really be more careful who you work with. So, spill it, Cyril. Now!"

He looked pretty spooked, but still didn't speak. "Let's have it Cyril."

I looked him in the eye. He was sweating. He was scared for sure. "Malkor Smeel."

"And they are?"

"Company manufacturing microchips in Taiwan for US Air Force weapons systems."

I was taken aback. I hoped it didn't show. "Anything else?"

"Malkor Smeel is owned by Tigran Gevorkian. He's Armenian from Yastavak."

It all sounded highly unlikely, but I sort of believed him. I couldn't see how a stupid guy like Goppis could be making that up. It required too much imagination to do that on the fly.

"And where can I find him?"

"In Scotland."

"Where?"

"Dunno . . . exactly. Never told me."

"So who does know?"

Goppis didn't reply. He stared out of the window. I got up slowly, walked over to him and held the muzzle to his head. "Spill it, Goppis." He didn't respond so I threatened to smack him with the barrel of the automatic.

He caved. I was surprised how quickly I wore him down. "Cherokee Jim."

"You taking the piss, Goppis?"

"No. I mean it. Cherokee Jim. He's a genuine Cherokee."

"So, where is he? North fucking Carolina or maybe Oklahoma?"

"No, here in the UK . . . in Brighton."

"Phone number?"

"07760 334433."

"You better not be lying, Goppis. Some of my people will stay in London. You will never be out of their sight. You got that?"

He threw open his hands, palms outwards.

"Those two hoods made a really big mistake when they took me on, Cyril my boy. They had no idea what kind of a shit storm would be coming down on them." I got up and, keeping the automatic trained on him, walked over to the window. I glanced through the curtains and nodded to the man, who wasn't there. I bent down and pulled his phone line right off the wall, crushing the connector under my heel. "Now your mobile. Put it on the table beside you and slide it over here."

He pulled out a phone and slid it over to me. I pocketed it. "And the other one."

"What other one?"

"Don't mess around, Goppis. Where the fuck is it?"

He sighed again. "Over there." He pointed to a table by the door. "Top left hand drawer."

I walked over to the table, keeping the automatic trained on the dispirited Cyril. I slid the drawer open and hooked out an old-looking unit, pocketing that too.

"That number again."

"07760 334433."

Using his best phone, I dialed and waited. A thick American voice came on the line. "Hello."

"Cherokee Jim?"

"Who is this?"

"Friend of Cyril Goppis."

"Is he with you?"

"Yup."

"Put him on the line."

With my hand over the phone, I looked at Goppis. "He wants to speak to you. Be very, very careful what you say. Tell him he should meet me. Be good for business. Got it?"

Goppis nodded. I went over to him, handed him the phone and pushed the barrel of the automatic against his skull.

"Hi, Jim . . . Yes, this guy's OK . . . Sure . . . He's got some business he could put our way . . . Where d'you want to meet him?"

Goppis listened then closed the line and passed the phone back to me. "Brighton. Slopes Road. Friday noon at The Flying Horse. Upstairs Lounge Bar."

"Good boy, Cyril. You've been most helpful."

He nodded.

"I'm going to go now, Cyril. If you breathe a word of my visit to anyone we'll get you. Is that clear?"

"Yes, that's clear."

As I left the building naturally enough I started to mull things over. I wondered what the hell people like that could want with my computer, phone and wallet. Then it dawned on me. They only wanted my computer. The phone and the wallet were taken to stop me calling the cops or telling anyone else for the few minutes it took them to make their getaway. It started to make some sense. But the computer? I couldn't see any purpose at all in taking that old heap of junk.

Chapter Nine

CHEROKEE JIM

**"Chance is the pseudonym of God
when he did not want to sign."
Anatole France**

I had leased a big sweet, silver Mercedes-Benz CL500 and I drove down to Brighton. I felt pretty damned cool in my sharp Ravello suit, white silk shirt and all.

The Flying Horse was a smart new-style pub and it was busy, but it wasn't hard to spot Cherokee Jim. He was the biggest man in the pub, dark-skinned and dangerous with long black hair and an impressively hooked nose. As I approached him, he eyed me cautiously, looking me up and down, clearly summing me up. I slid into the seat opposite him. "Hi, Jim. I'm John. We spoke on the phone."

He grunted and took a slow, calculated swig of his beer.

"What's your offer?"

"My offer?"

"Goppis said you had some business for us."

"Yes, I have Jim."

"And it is?"

I took out a roll of 20s and flashed it. He clocked the money and I had his full attention. "Tigran Gevorkian. Goppis told me he was in Scotland and that you knew exactly where."

Jim rocked back in his seat. "Ah, now, that's a tough call, Mr Smith. He's a dangerous man."

"I know that. So how much?"

He thought this over. "Five grand."

I whistled and took my time, playing the game. "Three."

"No, five, John."

"I'll just get a drink." I walked over to the bar and brought back a coke. I knew I had him and that he had what I wanted.

"OK, Jim. You got it. Five." I counted the notes out under the table and passed them across to his big, eager hand. I waited while he carefully counted the money. When he was done he looked up. His mind was made up. "Loch Inver. A big house overlooking the sea."

"Called?"

"Drumrunnie. You'll have to walk the last half mile. The track's too rough to drive."

I was pleased with myself. I had what I wanted again.

"I'm heading back to the States as soon as I can fix a flight, John. Lie low for a while. I don't want to be around when the Armenian realises who gave you the tip off."

"Fair enough, Jim. Makes sense. I won't tell him, of course."

"OK. But he'll figure it out any which way."

"Ever come across a couple of weirdos who go by the names of Nothing and Everywhere?"

Jim frowned and pondered. The names seemed to ring a bell. "Big hairy guy, small, skinny guy with quirky voices?"

"Yeah, that's them. Where can I find them?"

"Drumrunnie. Most likely. They bodyguard and run numbers for the Armenian."

Things were looking even brighter. I decided there and then to go for backup and to ask Biro to travel north with me.

"You've been very helpful, Jim. 'Preciate that. Have a good flight and the rest of your life."

We shook hands and I went back to my car, where I sat for a while considering my uncertain future. I had butterflies in my stomach, wondering what lay in store for me and if I really had the balls to see it though. I was hoping Biro would come with me and that he could get himself a gun. I had the money, but not the contacts. The drive back to London was painful. There had been a pile-up on the motorway and the traffic north was crawling through one lane round the wrecks. All the rubbernecking didn't help much either.

Chapter Ten

SUSIE BELLAVISTA

"In the pleasant days of summer,
Of that ne'er forgotten summer,
He had brought his young wife homeward
From the land of the Dacotahs;
When the birds sang in the thickets,
And the streamlets laughed and glistened,
And the air was full of fragrance,
And the lovely Laughing Water
Said, with voice that did not tremble,
'I will follow you my husband!'"
From The Song of Hiawatha
Henry Wadsworth Longfellow

I had arranged to meet Biro for breakfast after I'd picked up some things for the journey north, on which I was going to propose he join me. I was on my way when I spotted Comb-over crossing the street and coming towards me. He waved. He looked tired and dishevelled. His suit was strangely tighter than ever. A keen breeze lifted his hair and flopped it across his head, revealing his shining pate. He grabbed it, flipped it back across his skull and held it down. I stopped and waited while he sidled up to me.

"Morning, Mr Smith. I was on my way to pay you a call."

"What's up?"

"I met up with a couple of . . . er . . . underworld contacts last night and I made some progress on your case." He paused. I waited.

"One of them, a fella who goes by the name of Amos K R said he could help you, said he wanted to help you, but wants to meet you personally. Doesn't want to deal through me. Won't deal through me. I have to respect that."

"So?"

"He gave me his address to hand onto you." Comb-over fished through his pockets and after much scrimmaging eventually came up with a notebook, which he thumbed through. The pages flapped in the wind. His hair made another leap. His hands were busy so he just had to let it fly. He found what he wanted, drew out a ratty scrap of paper and handed it to me.

I took it from him and gave it a glance. "Thanks." I made to walk on.

"D'you have a number yet?"

"Nah. Haven't got around to it."

"Well . . . er . . . good luck with Amos, Mr Smith."

He grabbed his hair and slapped it down. We parted company and I made off down the street. I was transferring the paper to my top pocket when a gust lifted it clear of my hands and it danced off down the street. I gave chase, ducking and weaving, scattering pedestrians left and right. I kept the scrap in sight. I saw it fly right up to a pair of white sneakers then hover and drop. White Sneakers put a foot on it. I almost collided with her. I was stunned . . . it was . . . I smiled, she smiled and I dropped to my knees to retrieve the note from under her shoe, which she lifted slowly while I slid my hand underneath and grabbed it. White bobby socks. Brown shapely legs. I stood up as gracefully as I could and found myself face-to-face with a vision in a floral print cotton dress. Wavy honey-blonde hair, brown eyes, white teeth, Lips like a heart and slightly bee-stung. I attempted another smile.

She smiled back and I was opening my mouth to say sorry when she spoke. "Hi, that was impressive."

"Ah. Really so very sorry. It's an address . . . very important."

"That's OK. You can calm down now you've got it." She was American.

If only, I thought. I didn't know how to respond. I was speechless then finally managed to splutter out, "Can I buy you a coffee?"

She looked straight at me for a few seconds before she replied. "I wouldn't say no to that."

I couldn't believe she was being so friendly and open. British reserve, I guess.

We walked down the street a little way. Excusing myself, I called Biro and told him I would be a late.

I ordered two coffees and, as we waited, she told me her name was Susie, Susie Bellavista. Cool, I thought. Very cool.

"I'm afraid to admit that I'm just John Smith. I know it couldn't be more boring. But your name is outstanding and . . . er . . . unusual."

"It's not my real name. Well, Susie is, but I changed my second name to something I liked and could actually live with."

"What was it?" I was taken aback by my bluntness, but she wasn't fazed.

"Ah well . . . Bottomflight. I kept the 'B', but lost the rest of it."

I couldn't contain a snigger.

"I know it's awful. Easy to see why I changed it."

"Sure is."

"As a matter of fact it's an inaccurate translation of a Chinook Indian name. It had something to do with making arrows. Way, way back an ancestor of mine on my father's side was a Chinook. Must've been an arrow maker. The tribe lived along the shores of the Columbia River."

While I was watching her telling me this I went into a gentle trance. I could understand what she was saying without listening. The coffees arrived and I followed her to a table by the window. I was wondering who this girl was—actress, rock star, model, what? "D'you live in London?" I asked as nonchalantly as I could.

"Yup. For two years now."

"D'you like it here?"

"Not so much, but my work is here."

I was intrigued and just had to ask, "What is your work, Susie?"

"Pure math."

I could hardly believe my ears. "You're a mathematician!"

"That's right, John."

"Wow. I'm impressed and, I admit, I'm surprised."

"Why are you surprised?"

"Well, I . . . er . . ."

"Yes?"

"I . . . thought you were probably a movie star, Susie!'

She laughed. "Why'd you think that?"

"Well, your looks and all."

"Typical male reaction that, John."

"Sorry."

"You don't have to apologise. Sometimes it gets a little tiresome."

"Well, yeah, I guess it could."

There was an awkward silence. "So where d'you study?"

"I'm not a student, John. I'm a professor."

"You kidding?"

"No. Why would I kid you?"

"I dunno. No reason."

"Look, John. I was a bit of a prodigy. I passed the college entrance exams when I was 15. Went to Yale. Then Cambridge. I teach and research at UCL now."

"Wow! I'm impressed. In fact I'm very impressed."

"Well, you don't have to be. It's just a job."

"Sounds like more than a run-of-the-mill job to me, Susie."

"It's not really."

"What's your area of research?"

"*Number* Theory in general. Cyclotomic Fields in particular."

I must have looked dumbstruck because she went on, "Like I said, John, it's just a job. No need to be impressed."

I was though. Very.

"So tell me what you do, John?"

I felt myself curl up inside. "I'm a writer."

"Oh. Now that does sound exciting. What kind of writer?"

"Novels."

"Would I have read any?"

"Unlikely since I've never had anything published," I replied feeling ashamed.

"Really, nothing?"

"Well, OK. A couple of short stories, poems and I've done a smattering of journalism. Nothing you'd have seen or remember."

"Are you writing anything now?"

"I was." I felt a wave of grief pass through me and I shuddered.

"What d'you mean?"

And I found myself telling her the story. Just the robbery, though. Not the briefcase part.

She laughed when I told her what the hoods called themselves.

"Well, I guess it is funny in one sense. But not in the sense that I've lost my entire novel."

"Are you trying to get it back?"

"Of course." I told her about my first meeting with Comb-over at the cop shop but not about the second one. I told her too about having Biro's help, which reminded me that I was late to meet him. I didn't tell her how I met him.

"I have to see Biro now. Just around the corner, but I'm a bit late."

"That's fine. I have to give a lecture in an hour."

I struggled to pull myself and my courage together. I could hardly look at her. "Can we meet again later? Have dinner?"

"Yes, why not."

"Wow, wow, wow and Jesus H Christ," I thought to myself.

"Shall I pick you up, say, around 6:00?"

"Fine for me."

"Where?"

"I'll be outside the Math Department at 25 Gordon Street. It's up by Euston Station."

"Don't worry, Susie. I'll find it. I drive a Mercedes. It's silver."

"Lovely."

We got up to leave and parted company outside. I carried on to my meeting Biro, only looking back at her a couple of times. The second time she saw me and waved. I was walking on air. I was transformed.

Chapter Eleven

INSTANT KARMA

**"Instant Karma's gonna get you,
Gonna knock you right on the head.
You better get yourself together,
Pretty soon you're gonna be dead.
What in the world you thinking of,
Laughing in the face of love?"
John Lennon**

Biro was in his green suit again. In my Armani I felt I was on an equal footing.

"How're things, Biro?"

"OK. How 'bout you?"

I was bursting to tell him about Susie, but decided to contain myself and deal with the Armenian first. "I saw Goppis and persuaded him to tell me who those two clowns were working for."

"And?" Biro leaned forward. He really wanted to hear this.

"Tigran Gevorkian."

"Who's he?"

"An Armenian, who runs an outfit called Malkor Smeel. They make microchips for US Air Force weapons systems."

"Jesus!"

"Yeah, Biro. It's pretty amazing."

"What the hell has this got to do with your computer?"

"That is the question, my friend. That is it."

Biro was silent for half a minute. "D'you know where to find them?"

"Yup. I do. His plant is in Taiwan but he's in Scotland now and I know exactly where to find him."

"Holy shit!" Biro leaned back in his chair. I could see his mind was spinning. "How'd you find all this out?"

"Goppis told me about a guy in Brighton, who knew the address. I went to see him and persuaded him to tell me."

"How'd you do that?"

"Paid him five grand, Biro."

"Where the hell d'you get that kind of money?"

I told him about the briefcase I had found in the skip. I wondered if he'd believe me. I didn't tell him how much cash I had come by, but I did tell him about the Sig-Sauer and how I had used it to untie Goppis' slippery tongue.

"I'm impressed, John. I didn't take you for a violent man."

"I'm not, Biro. But I want my book back. Stealing it was unjust and I *will* find out why those two hoods took my computer. That's what I want to get to the bottom of."

"Well, you have to face the fact that you're really gonna be up against it with the Armenian."

"*We're* really up against it, Biro. Aren't you still with me on this one?"

"Yes, John. Sorry to have put it like that. I am still with you one hundred percent."

"As I understand it there's someone else who wants to help us."

"Who's that?"

"Someone who goes by the name of Amos K R. Ever heard of him?"

"Nope. How'd you come by him?"

"Tip off came from the cops. From the one I call Comb-over?"

"Strange. Why's he want to help us? What's in it for him?"

"No idea, Biro. But, as they say, never look a gift horse in the mouth."

As we left the pub I thought of Susie and experienced a warm, deep glow and felt myself spread out, filling the whole world. As we drove across town I told Biro about her. He listened patiently.

"I'll tell you this. She's very beautiful. She's American—from Kentucky and she's a maths professor at UCL."

"No shit."

I could see I'd got him wondering. I let it sink in.

"Are you sure she's not bullshitting you?"

"Why should she?"

"To make an impression."

"Why would she want to make an impression on me, Biro?"

"You have a very nice suit!"

Chapter Twelve

DEAD LINE

**With nothing material to lock prisoners behind
in the American Civil War the Confederate Army
gathered their captives together and drew a line
round them on the ground. Any prisoner who
strayed across this line was shot.**

When Biro and I forced our way into Amos' tiny, bare and
disgusting flat we were in for a big surprise. It was very quiet.
Something felt odd. We went from room to room. We finally
found him stone cold dead on the kitchen floor. He had been
shot. There was a shattered pane in the kitchen window. We
surmised that he had been killed from the rooftop opposite as
the glass shards had fallen inwards across the floor. There was an
envelope with my name still clutched in Amos' hand. I prised it
free.

Biro and I made a hasty exit, touching nothing else. I wiped
the handles of the doors and anything else we might have touched
on our way out. My heart was pounding as we took the stairs
down two steps at a time. Once outside we sauntered casually to

the Mercedes and sped off. I drove a mile or so then stopped the car to open the envelope. Biro watched me intently. I tried to breathe deep and slow.

Inside were two keys and a note. I read it out to Biro. "It's a name and an address in Brixton. Simpson. Ground floor flat. 16 Lion Square. "Let's go."

I drove carefully through the thick traffic. "Would you please put your safety belt on Biro. It's the law."

He ignored me.

We found a parking space after circling the streets for a couple of minutes. I fed the meter. Going up to the front door I thought of Susie again and my heart flew.

We let ourselves into the building and Biro opened the flat door. We entered a dimly lit hallway. The first door on the left was ajar. I went in. At first glance there was nothing unusual. TV, DVD player, glass-topped coffee table carrying two dirty mugs and an overflowing ashtray. Three-piece suite. Some books and DVDs. Then I saw the briefcase. It was leaning against one of the chairs. It was black with my initials embossed in gold on the lid. I walked over to it and picked it up without a second thought. I walked out of the room, calling to Biro that I was leaving, and out of the front door. I strolled back to the car, got in and shoved the case half under my seat.

Biro climbed in beside me. He looked from me to the briefcase and sat back. He put on his seat belt.

We drove out to the reservoir at Tottenham Hale and parked up in a quiet spot. I opened the case. I was less nervous the second time around. Inside was a white polystyrene block with a black leather pouch nestling in a cavity. I pulled out the pouch and opened it. It was a gun. There was also a note. I read it out to Biro:

"This Beretta has the edge on the Sig-Sauer. Handle with care. It's loaded."

We looked at each other. It was unnerving. I felt weak at the knees. I mean, who the hell could know we already had a Sig-Sauer. I sensed I was a pawn in someone else's game. Biro didn't look too happy either. I shoved the automatic back in the pouch and closed the briefcase pushing it back under my seat. We drove north towards Hampstead, not saying much, just thinking. Did anyone see me find the first briefcase? Had my house been searched? I doubted it. I concluded that it must be Goppis. I ran it by Biro and he agreed. Some questions remained unanswered: why did Amos want me to have the Beretta, what else was he planning to tell me and where did he fit into the picture?

"Things are getting a bit scary, Biro. Do you want out?"

He shrugged. "No way, man. I made a commitment. It's not my way to let people down. Anyway, life was getting boring."

"Well, it sure isn't now. We'd better watch our backs. We should move into a hotel and I'll lease another car. This one needs a clean in any case." I parked in a side street and called the leasing company, arranging to make the change in an hour. I looked down at the case and then across to Biro. "I think we have an operational problem."

"How's that, John?"

"I need a false identity."

"Why?"

"I want something—a fake passport—for checking into hotels. Things like that. D'you have any contacts for counterfeit documents?"

Biro thought about this "Yes, I know where to go, John. But it'll cost you."

"That's not an issue, but I want it in 24 hours."

"That'll cost a bit more."

"How much, Biro?"

"Five grand'll cover it."

"Let's do it."

"First move mug shots then. There's a Tesco store in Seven Sisters with a photo booth."

We drove over there and found a space in the car park. Biro waited while I went in and did the shots. I wasn't too pleased with the results, but handed the snaps to Biro when I got back to the car. He looked at them and laughed.

"Come on, Biro, they're not that bad."

"Guess not. They'll do."

I looked at him in enquiring kind of way.

"Yes, I've fixed it up, John. They can do a passport by this time tomorrow if I get the shots to 'em by 6.00."

On the way to the leasing company we stopped by my house and I picked up the cash. I googled the London Hilton and booked two rooms in my own name.

"What name d'you want on the passport?"

I gave this some consideration. "Wheat Trailer. I'll be Wheat Trailer. How's that?"

Biro laughed again. "Yes, Mr Trailer. That's an interesting name."

I handed him the cash then pulled away from the curb and headed off.

"You know what, John, you're a poet."

"Once a writer, always a writer. And you're a saint, Biro."

He laughed and I thought of my guru. I glanced at my watch. My heart fluttered. Just two hours until I picked up Susie.

We drove in contemplative silence until we reached the leasing company. I pulled into the yard and turned to Biro.

"I'll meet you at the Hilton at 11:00. Bring a toothbrush." I pressed an extra couple of hundred into his hand.

"You don't have to, John."

"I don't have to, Biro, but I want to. Really."

"OK. Thanks. See you later." He hailed a cab and was gone. Just for a moment I wondered if he was on the level. I shrugged. I trusted him. I wanted to. I needed to.

The car was ready and I went shopping. A bag shop and M&S for all the essentials. I would risk picking up my other suits tomorrow. I had half an hour to kill so I cruised round Soho looking for an expensive restaurant that took my fancy. I liked the look of Le Ciel d'Or. I googled them, got the phone number and booked a table for 6:30, remembering I was Wheat Trailer. I realised I would have to explain this to Susie. In any case I wanted to tell her more about what was going on—the money, the automatics, everything. I would tell her that I was going to have to go away for a few days. Probably tomorrow. Definitely tomorrow. I wondered how she would take it. Maybe it would be curtains for our relationship. I pulled myself up. Relationship? I realised I was getting a bit carried away, jumping the gun—appropriately—somewhat. But, positive waves I thought.

She was outside the Maths Department as I pulled up. Wow, she was gorgeous. I jumped out and opened the passenger door for her. She slid in and patted the seat. I went round to the driver's side and sat next to her.

"Nice car."

"Isn't it."

"Yours?"

"Not exactly, Susie. I lease it."

She nodded. "Where're we going?"

"Le Ciel d'Or. It's in Soho."

We drove sedately up to the West End and I put the car in the multi-storey. As we walked to the restaurant I took the bull by the horns. "I've booked us in under an assumed name."

"Assumed name! Why?"

"Well, it's like this Susie." I struggled to find the right words to begin my explanation. "I'm afraid that the people who stole my computer may be after me now."

"Why?"

"Because I'm after them and they want to stop me."

"How do you know that they're aware you're after them?"

I thought for a while before I replied. "I can answer that. I think. But I don't want to compromise you by telling you stuff you might find hard to keep to yourself. I mean, we've only just met and you're a professor and all . . ." I tailed off.

"I really want to know and I can keep a secret. I'm intrigued. So, tell me."

"Well, it could be a coincidence I guess, Susie, but I had an appointment to meet a shady character today called Amos K R. I had been told that he wanted to meet me. I got the impression that he had something for me, information or some such."

"Who told you this?"

"The cops."

"The cops!"

"Yes, well, one cop in particular. Detective Sergeant Grimsthorne."

"What's this Grimsthorne up to, John?"

"He's the one who interviewed me about the burglary."

"Yes. OK. But what's he up to?"

"What d'you mean, Susie?"

"I mean, don't you think it strange that he gives you the name of a criminal, who wants to meet you? Seems a kinda fishy to me."

"Maybe. I don't know. I get the impression that he works with informers—grasses—that kind of thing."

"Still doesn't make sense. Just wonder what he's really up to."

We walked on in silence. I didn't know what to say. Put like that it did all sound a bit suspect.

We turned into Greek Street and I led Susie across the road to Le Ciel d'Or. A waiter opened the door for us.

"I've booked a table for two. Wheat Trailer."

Susie giggled. It was charming.

We took our seats. "Wheat Trailer! Are you kidding?" She was laughing. I took this to be a positive sign.

"Good name, don't you think?"

"It's good. I like it. Very creative."

"Thank you. As a matter of fact the first name that sprang to mind was Tractor Trailer, but that was, I dunno, just too much."

Susie laughed again like water tumbling down a mountain stream. The waiter came over with menus and a wine list.

I took the wine list and handed it to Susie.

She looked surprised. "Don't you want to choose?"

"No, not really. I don't drink and I haven't a clue about wine."

She smiled at me again. "Then I won't have any either." She turned to the waiter, "Just a bottle of sparkling water, please."

He took the wine list away. I smiled at Susie. We looked at our menus. I scanned through mine for the vegetarian options. I didn't want to make a big deal about my diet in case I came across as too cranky, what with not drinking and all. She was looking through her menu and then glanced up at me.

"There're some nice dishes on here but I don't really like meat too much these days so I'll start with something light and then maybe have some fish for the main course."

So we got through ordering without any issues coming up but I'm sure she noticed that I didn't have anything with meat, fish or eggs. When the waiter left us she looked me in the eye and asked directly, "So J . . . Wheat what d'you plan to do next?"

"About what?" I asked as innocently as I could.

"About getting your book back, silly."

"Ah, yes the book. Well, I have to get the computer it's on back."

"So, what's your next move?"

"Well, Susie, I think I know exactly where it is."

"Exactly?"

"Yes, exactly where it is." She put her head to one side. My heart felt mushy and my mouth was dry. "I . . . er."

"Yes?"

I took a sip of water and looked down at my plate, steadying myself. I lowered my voice "It's in Scotland. Up on the northwest coast."

"How come?"

"It's where the two thieves and their boss hang out."

"Are you sure?"

"As sure as I can be about anything in this crazy mess." Our starters were served and I had a break while we enjoyed the food. I looked up at Susie, "Is it OK?"

"It's lovely, thank you, Wheat."

"Mine too."

As the waiter took away our plates, she asked, "Are you going to tell me anymore?"

"'Bout what?"

"Scotland."

"What's there to say?"

"Well, for a start, what are you going to do, John?"

I could see I was going to have to tell her more or less the whole thing."

"In essence my friend Biro and I are going to drive up there and attempt to retrieve my computer."

"Where's there?"

"Loch Inver. A big house overlooking the sea. It's called Drumrunnie."

"And who's there?"

"An Armenian gangster from Yastavak called Tigran Gevorkian and I guess those two henchmen Nothing and Everywhere.

Gevorkian owns a company called Malkor Smeel which makes microchips for US Air Force weapons systems. My guess is that this is only a part of their operations and that they're into other and even more shady things."

Susie thought about this. She kept her voice down when she did eventually speak again. She leaned in close to me. I was blissed but just managed to stay focused.

"There must've been something on that machine of yours that they wanted."

"What on earth could that be? I had a few applications, letters, emails, my writing. Nothing of interest to anyone else. Except, of course, my porn."

"Pornography?"

"Not really. Just joking. There wasn't any."

"I'm glad to hear it."

"Not my thing."

"Good" The dear girl looked relieved.

"How could whatever it is they wanted be on my computer, Susie? It doesn't make sense."

"It doesn't. I agree."

"Whatever it is or was, I have to get my novel back." I told her the story of T. E. Lawrence and how that completely spooked me. She got my point.

"So when're you going?"

"Soon as possible. Probably tomorrow night."

"I want to come with you, John."

This really threw me. "You're kidding. Why?"

"I need some excitement."

"Wow, Susie! You are kidding me. I mean isn't your job exciting?"

"Up to a point, John, but I'm not really at the leading edge. I'm just not coming up with anything new. I want to do that, but I'm not and it's frustrating. I expected much more of myself. I thought I would have made some great discovery by now."

I felt pretty much the same. I had expected to be an acclaimed and successful author by the time I made 35.

The waiter served our main course. We were silent until he had moved out of earshot. We continued, keeping our voices down.

"It's going to be exciting all right, Susie, but it could also be very dangerous. Remember I told you that Nothing and Everywhere were armed. Well, Everywhere was at least. My guess is there'll be a lot more guns at that house."

"If that's true, how're you and Biro going to take them on?"

I didn't know what to say. Should I tell her about our guns? I pondered then decided to dive right in.

"We've got guns too, Susie . . . and a little ammunition."

"Holy shit! You never cease to surprise me. Everyone has guns in the US but here it's a different matter."

"Agreed."

"So where'd you get them?"

"It's a long story, Susie."

"So, tell me."

"OK, but let's eat." I tried to move sideways on the gun issue. "Do you have a . . . ?"

"No. No husband, boyfriend or girlfriend come to that, just now."

I could hardly believe it. Such a beautiful, gifted woman. I knew I shouldn't put myself down, but why me?

She cut up her food delicately and then glanced up at me. "I was married once, but that all fell apart a while back. How about you?"

"No one at the moment. I split up with my girlfriend a few months back." We looked at each other. Some understanding passed between us. We smiled. It was so . . . sweet.

"What about your work? Can you take time off, Susie?"

"Yes, I can. I'm scheduled for a three-week sabbatical starting Monday, but I could go early. My boss is pretty flexible."

My heart was pounding. I couldn't believe that she would want to go away with me and on such a strange journey.

"So what about these guns, John?"

"Uhmmm." I didn't know what to say or where to start. "We got one off Amos K R. A Beretta. He was dead by the time we got to him, but he left me some keys and an address where I found yet another briefcase with my initials. It was inside."

"And the other . . . ?"

"Later, Susie. OK?"

"OK, we can leave that for now."

I breathed a silent sigh of relief. The money was causing me some grief. It was a lot to explain and made me guilty. My guru flashed across my mind again. I flushed.

Chapter Thirteen

OPENING THE HEART

"Some of us never learn to take orders."
Michael Crichton

We picked up the Mercedes from the multi-storey and on the way to Susie's flat in Finsbury Park I made this observation. "Remember the film *Bonnie and Clyde?*"

"Sure."

Remember C.W. Moss?"

"He drove the getaway car, as I recall."

"So that's you, Susie." Biro and I go in alone. You wait in the car. That a deal?"

"OK, John. I'll settle for that. You're the boss."

We drove on in silence for a while. "Where d'you come from, Susie?"

"I was born and grew up in Jackson County, Kentucky."

"I've never met anyone from Kentucky before. The Bluegrass State isn't it? Famous for horses, as I recall."

"That's right."

"So what was it like, Susie?"

"Well in Jackson County—very conservative, very republican and mostly very poor. I couldn't wait to get away."

"Anything good about it?"

"Sure, the famous race horses, yes, and the bluegrass around Lexington. And South of Lexington, Berea College attracted a lot of left-leaning professors. It was very liberal. So I fitted in there pretty well."

"Anything else?"

"That not enough, John?"

"It's a good start."

"Well, yes, there were several other things." She slipped away a bit, reflecting.

"Like what?"

"Like the world's longest cave system, the greatest length of navigable waterways in the United States, the largest free-ranging *elk* herd east of Montana, skilled artisans right across the state, mountain musicians, a strong sense of kith and kin. How 'bout that?"

"Well, Susie, sounds good to me."

"And you?"

"Not very interesting. I was born in North London and I still live there." We drove on in silence for a while. When we reached Finsbury Park Susie directed me to her flat. I pulled up outside. I looked across at her, "Shall I pick you up tomorrow then?"

"Yeah, let's do it." She clapped her hands. "Let's kick ass."

I laughed and so did she. "What time?"

"Whenever you like."

"Say, about 6:00. I'll be packed."

"And I'll be there—armed and ready!" I chuckled and she gave me the sweetest smile I had ever seen.

"If you don't mind me saying so, Susie, you're a real cool girl."

"And you're a real sweet guy, John." She unbuckled her seat belt and leaned over towards me. I turned to her and she gave me a soft and gentle kiss on the lips. I kid you not, she smelt of new-mown hay. I guess I realised then that I was in love and what a feeling that was. Nothing like it in this world.

Biro and I stayed that night at The Hilton.

Chapter Fourteen

UNITED WE STAND, DIVIDED WE FALL

Motto of the State of Kentucky

I packed my bag, took out another 20 grand, the Sig-Sauer and the spare magazine. I stuffed the cash into my jacket pocket. I wrapped the gun and the mag in one of my shirts, taped round them and put them in my bag at the bottom. After I had picked up my other suits I drove over to The Hilton and asked a porter to watch my car as I was only going to be a few minutes. Biro was waiting in the foyer, wearing his apple green suit. He looked good. I checked us out and we left. I remoted the boot open. Biro put his bag inside, walked round the car and climbed into the passenger seat.

I tipped the porter a large one. He almost bowed with thanks. I climbed into the driver's seat beside Biro.

"OK, John." We shook hands. "Let's rock."

I put the Mercedes in gear and we cruised off up to Finsbury Park.

"Susie's coming with us."

"Huh?"

"She's up for it and she's very bright."

"A girl, though . . . is that wise?"

"Wait 'til you meet her, Biro."

"Can't wait, John." He sounded resigned and glanced at me sideways. He looked skeptical.

It was raining. I put the a/c and the wipers on.

"How many rounds you got for that Beretta, Biro?"

"Full mag. Fifteen."

"That's 39 rounds between us. Should make something of an impression."

"Should do." He paused and looked across at me, "Are you nervous, John?"

"Yeah, sure, I'm nervous. Excited too, I guess, Biro. Never done anything remotely like this before."

"Me neither."

"Well, it makes a change then." We laughed. It continued to rain.

A few minutes later I was ringing the bell to Susie's flat and waited in the drizzle. She wasn't long. She was wearing jeans and a leather jacket. She looked dressed for the business. Taking her bag, I opened the nearside rear door. She slid in and Biro turned to greet her. I saw his jaw drop visibly. He blinked. I put her bag in the boot and climbed into the driver's seat.

"Hello, Biro. I've heard all about you."

"Not too much I hope. Not that there's a lot to tell."

"Enough to be going on with. I guess we'll learn a lot more about each other on the drive north."

"I guess we will." Biro glanced at me. I could see he was impressed. Interesting team, I thought, as I put the car in gear and we moved off. We took the A1M. I prefer it to the M1. Don't know why, after all they're just sodding motorways.

"We'll need to get some gas soon. Anyone fancy a cup of coffee?" They both said yes, almost in unison. It was a good sign and I was looking for good signs.

We gassed up, parked and went into the glaring, plastic cafeteria. I bought coffees and doughnuts. We sat at a table by a window and watched the traffic pounding and hissing by. It was still raining hard.

Susie looked up from her doughnut, "Why haven't you told Comb-over that you think you know where your computer is and who's got it, John?"

"I think he already knows and for some reason doesn't want to do anything about it."

"What makes you think that?"

"Well, like I told you, he put me onto Amos K R."

Biro took a sip of coffee. "My guess is he's bent and is on some kinda backhander."

Susie thought about this. "You could be right there, Biro. It would explain a lot."

We finished our snack in silence, went to the loo and back to the car in the rain. I put on my Best of Elvis CD to get on top of the weather and the boredom, not to say danger, of the motorway.

Biro was about to get into the front passenger seat, then thought better of it. "D'you want to sit next to John, Susie?"

"Yes, I do. Thanks."

We stopped for dinner in Leeds then drove on until 2:00am. I had Biro google us up a classy hotel in Newcastle. I flipped on the sat nav and we arrived there without getting lost. I booked us in separate rooms under my assumed name with my fake passport. We managed not to laugh with difficulty.

Susie was a real sport all right. Biro went up to his room immediately, agreeing to breakfast at 8:00. Susie and I sat in the lobby for five minutes. She told me she liked Biro and felt confident with him. I said I agreed. We discussed our next stop. I opened up my map App, remembering that I must charge the phone. We decided to stay at the Inver Lodge in Loch Inver, which to my reckoning was about 10 miles from Drumrunnie. We kissed goodnight and went to our rooms. That night I had an extraordinary dream.

Chapter Fifteen

DREAM TWISTER

**"You're a man of the mountains,
you can walk on the clouds
Manipulator of crowds,
you're a dream twister . . . . ."
Bob Dylan**

I was in India. In a city I'd never visited. It was hot. I was in one of those scooter-cabs—Vespas with tin boxes welded on the back. Tiny seats, no safety belts—scuttling through the traffic and fumes. Everyone was on mobile phones and the sky was full of choppers, blasting away at each other with missiles, rockets and machine guns. Aircraft were falling out of the sky in flames all over the city, which was slowly turning into a raging inferno. No one seemed to care or pay this any attention. Cracks were starting to appear in the roads and sidewalks. Vehicles were just driving over them or round them. The pedestrians were doing more or less the same. A huge crack appeared in front of my taxi and we plunged down into the ground. A vast chasm opened up before me. I saw the scooter and the driver spin off into the void.

After falling and tumbling for what seemed like an age I started to rise up and all around me the space became diffused with swirling lights and colours. Stars twinkled and sparkled through it all. My ascent slowed and I came out on a verdant plane surrounded by purple mountains, capped with shining snow. I was propelled towards a golden temple. As I entered beautiful and transcendent music cascaded all around me. I saw a throne ahead of me and on that throne sat my guru. He was meditating. Love suffused him. His face was a glowing picture of divine bliss. Across his knees lay a black and shining AK47 assault rifle.

I woke up. Puzzled, but feeling good. Inspired. I concluded that I was doing the right thing on this quest and that I was on right track and with the right people.

Chapter Sixteen

THE TREE OF LIFE

**"Science without religion is lame.
Religion without science is blind."
Albert Einstein**

I woke early. I had heard that my favourite director, Terrence Malick, had a new film out called *The Tree of Life*. I thought we could do with some distraction. They had WiFi in the hotel so I booted up my new laptop and cruised around the net until I found that the film was showing at 10:00am at the Odeon Cinema in the Gateshead Metrocentre.

My favourite film is Malick's beautiful and moving *The Thin Red Line*. I saw it in LA late one night with Oscar. When we came reeling out of the cinema Oscar turned to me. I could see he had been crying. The final sequence was extremely harrowing.

"Well, John. One word I guess."

I nodded. I didn't need to say anything. Oscar did it for me: "Masterpiece."

And so it is, without a shadow of a doubt, an out-and-out masterpiece. The way Malick mixes in the purity and beauty of nature with the terrifying horrors of warfare. There's a remarkable sequence where a group of islanders walk silently past a platoon of sweating US grunts making their way towards a hill, which they have been tasked with taking by their embittered colonel. It would appear that the soldiers are all-but invisible to the scantily dressed islanders. There are many other striking shots like the cut-away to the blinking owl, sitting quietly and unmoved in a tree high above the trudging line-doggies, apparently unmoved by the shit-storm which is about to unfold. The allegory for life is perfect. The thrust of the story is about getting to the top of the hill and securing it against fearsome and determined odds. Just like life. Simple and clear.

I have now watched that film four times and it never ceases to amaze and impress me. Thank you, Mr Malick.

Another favourite film of mine is *Das Boot*. Another war film, but hey, I also love *Casablanca*. There was a story going around in LA, and I don't know how true it was, that a group of writers made an experiment. They submitted the screenplay of *Casablanca* to a bunch of studios under the title *Dinner at Ricks*. It was universally rejected!

Anyway I put the idea of taking in the film to the others at breakfast. There were no objections. In fact there was a fair amount of enthusiasm. Biro was unexpectedly another big fan of *The Thin Red Line*. We arrived on time and ground through the inevitable, inane and expensive commercials which were all—without exception—trying to persuade us to waste our money on useless junk. The ads for alcohol always made me cringe. The irony of glossy images of slick, shallow people getting pissed with the disclaimer at the end 'Please drink responsibly'. Jesus! Drink responsibly? It makes people stupid and sick. I rest my case. As far as I'm concerned they should make alcohol illegal and legalise cannabis. That really would make sense.

The Tree of Life was a bold film. Unlike the strong storyline of The Thin Red Line I felt this one never got going. There are some amazing images of the cosmos and nature. Malick wasn't in a rush. It's a study of people struggling with pain, disappointments and the woes of life etc. But I didn't really care about any of 'em except maybe the wife. Good acting, OK. Good dialogue,

OK. Amazing visuals, OK. But it didn't add up to much. Only Mr Malick could have got away with this.

It was also too long, which was why towards the end I had to go out for a pee. After I had done what I needed I walked out into the foyer to stretch my legs and there—surprise, surprise—was Comb-over. He had his back turned towards me so I saw him but he didn't see me. He was obviously not doing a good job of watching us but I was shaken. This was getting out of hand. I felt vulnerable and overwhelmed. I leaned back against the wall in the shadows to calm down and watch. Comb-over looked around and then at his watch. I was not sure what I should do. In the end I decided. I slipped back into the cinema.

As I was squeezing into my seat Biro's phone rang. He fumbled through his pockets desperately trying to get his hand on the offending machine. When he did find it, he dropped it and it scudded across the floor still ringing. There was a shout from the back, "Shut the fuck up. Wanker!" But that was as far as it went. Nobody came and actually punched him. Biro was embarrassed. Susie and I couldn't suppress a little giggle. It wasn't like Biro, who was usually so together. Ah, but I guess we're all flawed to a greater or lesser extent. It was a good thing that Malick wasn't with us! He would have been very pissed off too.

When the film finished and the credits had run we couldn't find the phone. In the end I broke out mine and called his number. We followed the sound and managed to retrieve it.

We went back to the hotel for lunch and left for Carlisle soon after we had eaten. The sun was still shining. We climbed away from the town in silence. I had an uncomfortable feeling. Thinking about Comb-over, I felt suddenly guilty for bringing Biro and Susie with me. I was painfully burdened with an oppressive and overwhelming responsibility for them, for the guns, everything. My commitment was wobbling. I was worried.

"Look, I just have to say I do not intend harm to anyone. The guns just put us on a par, that's all."

"As long as we're prepared to use them." Biro smiled. He meant it.

I stopped the car in a lay-by. The moor stretched out around us. Even in the sun it had a melancholy feel. Susie walked off alone. I tried to find a way through my conflicting opinions. I said to Biro, "I am prepared up to a point."

"And what does up to a point mean exactly? What point might that be and where is it?"

"I just hope it doesn't come to shooting. I won't be able to shoot anyone. I can shoot around . . ."

"What if they're shooting at you? Then what, John?"

"It depends."

"Depends on what?" Biro was clearly convinced of the rightness of the possibility of serious violence built into our rescue bid.

"Look," I responded weakly, "they were given to us as an equaliser, OK? We don't know how or why, but they really did fall into our laps. Not that that necessarily means they've come to us without a price."

We walked over to Susie. She had obviously been thinking and she addressed both of us, "Why did Comb-over put you onto Amos K R? What could have been in it for him?"

"The only thing is money." Biro replied quickly. "As I see it, he was part employed by Amos. Amos paid him for leaks. So he did what Amos asked him to do and gave you his number. So, who was Amos working for—that's the thing?" He didn't wait for a reply. "The same Armenians. That's where I put my money."

"Chances are that's it, Biro." I shook his hand. "Let's walk for an hour or so. OK?" They both nodded in agreement. I strode off with Susie beside me. The going was rough and we kept losing the path. When it came time to turn back we had to steer by the sun. It was still quite early when we got back to the car. We ordered an Indian take-away then we drove up to the restaurant and parked outside. The street was deserted. Eventually an overweight couple waddled by. Watching them made me feel fit. My mind drifted back into my dream. When I got a firm hold on it, it was as vivid and clear as ever. I don't know if it was all there in the recall. But it was impressive in any case. The final image of the guru with the gun was tricky even to attempt an interpretation. I hoped it was telling me OK. Get on with it. On the other hand, maybe the converse was the meaning of it. Two boys went by on skateboards with a clatter and a whoosh. I came back to our immediate situation. Why did Comb-over put us onto Amos I wondered? Why did Amos give us the Beretta? If it's a setup, who's setting up who? Who's working for whom?

"Time to eat," said Biro as he opened his door and climbed out. I came back to the present and followed him into the restaurant to collect the food.

Ten minutes later we spotted a picnic area. We pulled off the road and parked. There were wooden tables and chairs and the sun was still warm. It was a tranquil setting in a glade of trees with gentle hills rising up and away behind them. Apart from us there was no one else around. A dog barked sharply off in the trees. The smell of woodsmoke touched the air. We laid out the food and started to eat.

Biro told the story of his one visit to the United States ten years before. He had been working as a roadie for a Hungarian rock band doing a minor, cross-country tour. They played nearly every night in a different city for six weeks. Sometimes they played two gigs in one night at different venues. Mostly it went OK but it had been a rough trip and he didn't come away with a good impression of the USA. He was struck though by the national and state parks and wildernesses: the mountains, the deserts, the lakes and the forests. Susie's attitude was much more positive. She had good memories of growing up in Kentucky. She'd had a homely childhood in a stable family and had mostly got on well with her older brother and younger sister. Her father had a well-paid and steady job as a top school administrator. They were not rich but never short of money. Her mother was a much loved and respected kindergarten teacher.

Susie told us that her passion for mathematics started when she was eight. She had been browsing the popular science shelves in the municipal library one day and pulled out a book on maths history. She went through the index, found a chapter called 'Infinities' and thumbed through to the appropriate page. She read about the German mathematician Georg Cantor. He was best known as the inventor of *set theory*. This had become a *fundamental theory* in mathematics. Cantor established the importance of *one-to-one correspondences* between sets, defined *infinite* and *well-ordered sets*, and proved that the *real numbers* are more numerous than the *natural numbers*. In fact, she read,

Cantor's theorem implies the existence of an *infinity* of infinities. Susie intuited that this work implied something profound, but on another level—one she didn't understand until years later when she studied philosophy.

Georg Cantor had illustrated the idea of infinity to his students with a simple proposition: there was a hotel that had an infinite number of rooms and the hotel was always fully occupied. So when one more guest arrived the manager moved the guest in room one to room two, the guest in room two to three, the guest in three to four and so on. In this way room number one was always available to a new guest. She looked up 'sets' in the index. She could clearly remember the impact this reading had on her. One thing that stuck in her mind was the mind-blowing paradoxical question about sets posed by the quirky philosopher Bertrand Russell: 'Does the set of all sets, which don't contain themselves, contain itself?'

Susie had always excelled at arithmetic, learning in a day what took the other children in her class a week to pick up. She was lucky that when she was eight her teacher had the wit to see that she was in the presence of a very gifted child, a formidable talent. She recommended that Susie take on extra studies with a math tutor. Rudi Havenrichter was lecturing at the University of Kentucky. It only took him a little over an hour to drive down from Lexington to Jackson County. He met with Susie twice a week and sometimes more. He was staggered by her abilities and it inspired him to be with her so he went as often as he had the time. He couldn't always keep up with her, but he was most useful stopping her from wasting her time in dead ends and backwaters. He was the perfect guide for her on her journey through the dense, dark wood of numbers. And numbers are what most interested Susie. Numbers and infinity.

Biro and I were content to listen. I found it astonishing that I should be here, now with his extraordinary person. I had never, to my knowledge at least, had a special gift for anything. I was more or less mundane at everything at school. Having said that, I did develop a shallow interest in physics. I read a few lightweight 'popular' books on the subject. I started with Fritjof Capra's *The Tao of Physics* because he was seeking parallels between mysticism and quantum physics. I loved to read about Einstein. I had heard him say in a radio interview that 'science without religion is lame and religion without science is lame'. This struck a chord with me and he became my hero.

Susie looked off into the distance and paused, remembering. "Sometimes I felt like a freak, other times people would treat me differently from other kids. High school was OK. Well, I had the looks to help and I was popular. I did have a different schedule from anyone else while I pursued my number game and took on extra tutorials. I was interested by all those things like *Fermat's little theorem, Euler's theorem*, the *Chinese remainder theorem*, the law of *quadratic reciprocity* . . . . blah, blah, blah." She glanced up, clocked our uncomprehending looks and blushed. "Sorry . . . don't mean to blind you with science!"

"I like it," I replied. "It's a great story, even if I don't know the first thing about number theory, which I don't, Susie."

Biro grinned and gestured around him, "And I don't either, but this trip is turning out to be so much more than I ever expected."

The sun had all but set. We collected up our rubbish, binned it and got back on the road.

"I saw a TV doc about that Wiles guy, who solved Fermat's Last Theorem," I observed. "Took him years, just working away on his own. It's a wonder he didn't go mad."

Susie laughed. "Too many mathematicians do lose it, John. Later in life Cantor had many bouts of pitch-black depression, broken up with flying highs until he died. Andrew Wiles is sane. So some are all right and get through it." She smiled. It was too good to look at. I turned away.

My phone rang. I pulled over to the side of the road and switched off the engine. It was Comb-over. "Good evening, Detective Inspector. What's new? . . . I'm not in London . . . I'm driving north with friends . . . just a short break: nothing too ostentatious . . . . hold on with all the questions, man. What have you got for me? . . . it doesn't matter where I am . . . so, no new leads? . . . nothing. What about Amos? Nothing? . . . I gotta wonder what you're doing . . . so don't go on asking me what I'm doing. I'm not the detective. You are. Goodbye." I finished the call and handed the phone to Biro.

"Find us a hotel in Fort William, please. In the best of all possible worlds it's a 2½ hour drive."

He got through and booked three rooms in a nice-sounding establishment in the centre.

"The only thing Comb-over wanted to know was where I was and what I was doing. Strange." We drove on in silence for a while.

"I'll get another phone tomorrow. They might be able to track this one." I pulled the car over to the side of the road, got out, found a rock and crushed the phone. We got back on the road. The traffic was light and the scenery spectacular. White clouds raced across the sky. We arrived in good time for dinner.

The next day dawned fine and we were ready to leave early. "Do you want to drive, Susie?" I asked as we crossed the car park. "Biro doesn't. You might as well get used to it."

"I like to drive. And this car . . . uh huh."

I handed her the keys and climbed into the passenger seat. She pulled away from the hotel and easily found her way through town. She looked comfortable at the wheel and drove well. I wasn't surprised.

Just north of Carlisle we opted for the A74(M) to take us up to Glasgow. She kept to the speed limits. We didn't want anyone to notice us or get close to us—certainly not the cops. Biro tracked down a hotel and booked us in.

"I have a relative in Glasgow—my mother's brother." Susie turned to me. "Could we look him up?"

I glanced at Biro and he shrugged. "That's OK, Susie, if we just slip in and out quietly."

"D'you want Biro to call him for you?"

"It can wait. I'm enjoying the drive."

We met in reception later. Susie was studying a local map. "It's not far from here. Princes Square. We could walk."

I would have liked that, but it was not such a good idea, so I replied, "Safer to drive, I think."

"Better to keep as low a profile as we can," agreed Biro.

Chapter Seventeen

MARCH KLOSSOWSKI

"Let all mud be velvet."
Stash de Rola, 1967

I picked up a new phone and number as soon as the stores opened the next morning. I put it on charge in the car. As I drove through the city I found myself checking the rear view mirror more often. I had a feeling we were being followed. I hadn't any evidence, but I just felt it.

"My uncle March is a bit of a recluse. I wouldn't say eccentric . . . but . . . different. He's been living alone since my aunt died. He hasn't ever completely got over that. Now he doesn't really know anyone here. He should go back to the States but he won't listen."

"What does he do here?"

"Like you, John, he's a writer. Like you he's not really published."

"Oh, boy. Another one!" I felt a tearing pang for my book. I wanted it back. I wanted it in my hands. I needed it. I felt a red anger rising. I wriggled in my seat. "My book. I need my book. It is me!"

"Take it easy, John. We're going to get it back. Trust me." Biro patted my shoulder. Susie touched my hand.

We found a space near to the square and fed the meter. Susie climbed the steps to the front door and pressed the bell. Biro stared up at the building. "Is this whole house his?"

"Yes. He rattles around in there like a peanut in a bucket."

"Must be worth a fortune."

"Must be," Susie agreed.

The door opened and a little old man with a friendly, well-worn face in a Stetson swung it wide when he saw Susie.

"Darlin' girl. You've come to see me again. Bin a long time."

"I know, Uncle. I'm sorry . . . I've brought a couple of friends along too."

"Come on in."

Susie introduced us.

We followed him through the hall to the front sitting room. It was tidy, well furnished, but deep in dust. He waved us onto chairs.

"How you doing, Susie? D'you still like London?"

"I'm doing fine, thank you, Uncle. I like what I do and, yes, I do still like London enough to put up with it. Not as much as Paris or New York or Berlin, of course . . . but . . . what about you?"

"Oh, I'm same as ever. Grinding closer and closer to getting something else in print and staying fit. I'm writing a book about Kentucky in the 80s and 90s, more or less your childhood years. You might even read it! It takes a radical stand around corruption in State politics, though. So it might be too extreme." He sighed. "I guess you'd all like tea?" He looked round and saw we were positive. He stood. "I'll do it." He signalled to us to relax and left the room.

"The Kentucky book sounds worth reading especially if it is extreme. I guess you'd read it, Susie."

"I would, John. Be fascinating to get another view of those years."

"What does he usually write?"

"Uh. Hard to describe . . . good stories told with political motives. He is—was—more of an activist than a writer. He was refused entry back into the USA a decade ago but that ban has been lifted. He could go back."

Biro broke the silence, "He seems happy here. He must have some friends, surely?"

"I don't know. He always insists he hasn't. I've never seen anyone else here and he never talks about anyone he knows now. He has a great memory though. His books are historical. Well, they are as much about the era as they are about the people in the stories. They have never worked out for him, never hit the spot. Not a one."

I felt his pain. Susie glanced at me. "He once built up a good following as a journalist and very quickly. He was published a lot—in serious newspapers, magazines."

"What happened?"

"He dropped it to focus on his books."

March came back in with a big tray: cups, saucers, teapot, sugar, milk. He set it down, started to spread things out and poured the tea. "So where are you three headed?"

"To a place on the coast in northwest Scotland."

"Where exactly? I know that area well. Your aunt Lois and I walked a lot of it before she died. I haven't been back since, but I'd like to."

"Loch Inver."

"I know it well. It's a place I like. We were around there more than once."

I glanced over at Biro. It was another unexpected connection. He raised an eyebrow.

"Why are you going there?" March asked innocently.

"To collect some equipment."

"Must be unusual *equipment*," he responded.

"It is. It's unique. It is the only one of its kind in the world." March leaned towards me, "What is it?"

"It's a computer." I hoped this would be enough for him.

"Well, OK, it's a computer but what's on it, John?"

"I just couldn't help myself and out it came. "My book. It has the only copy there is of the novel I have just finished. I have to get it back."

"How come it's in Scotland, John?"

"We don't really know."

"But you know who has it?"

I nodded. "We think so."

"How did you lose it?"

"I didn't lose it, March. The machine was stolen."

"Ah, the plot thickens. Why?"

"We don't know. Probably not for my book." I smiled.

March looked excited. "I would like to come with you. I saw your car. You have enough room. What d'you think?"

"I can understand that you'd like to go back and see that country again, but . . ."

"But, what?"

"Could be dangerous."

"Why dangerous?"

"Well . . . it's all a little unpredictable. The thieves are probably armed and may not want to return my computer."

"What about you, John? You armed?"

I was taken aback by his bluntness. I looked at the others.

Susie leaned back in her chair, "They have two handguns, yes, March."

"Look, I just want to ask them to give me my computer back. Just for the book. That's all. The guns came our way. We did not go out looking for them. Never asked for them . . . it's odd, I know."

"Like I said, I would like to come with you. But now I *want* to come with you. I am determined to come with you."

I looked at him for an explanation."

"Great material. Fresh material for me."

"Hold on, March. You can't write about us," I responded sharply. "There's too much that can't be told. We hope that no one else knows we're here. We took a lot of care to ensure we weren't followed."

"I just need some raw material. I'll change the detail, the locations, the time, the people. Don't worry. If I write anything you can read it before I do anything with it. OK?"

I liked him and thought he would be just the right kind of travelling companion for this particular operation. I glanced at the others. They both nodded.

"OK, March. You can come with us."

"Good. I'll get ready. I need to make a couple of calls. I was going to the movies tomorrow night with a lady from across the street. It's no big deal. She'll understand."

There was something at the back of my mind trying to push itself up to the surface. "Binoculars!" I got it, jumped to the door and called up to March, "D'you have any binoculars?

March called down the stairs, "Yes, I have. I'll bring 'em."

I turned back into the room. "I kept forgetting those things when we've been shopping."

"Good thinking." Biro looked pleased.

"We should get to Fort William by lunch tomorrow and then it's 4 to 4½ hours to Loch Inver, which will be a spectacular ride."

We left the house and walked quickly back to the car.

As we drove off Biro asked, "Back there you said that we weren't followed. What did you mean?"

"Just what I said: we weren't followed."

"Why did you say it then? Maybe you've seen something?"

"What are you getting at, Biro?" I felt a wave of irritation.

He was silent for a few seconds. Then, "I wonder if you've seen anything that you haven't mentioned."

"Why would I do that, Biro?"

"Not to spread anxiety or maybe you just weren't sure."

Biro had caught the note of anger in my voice. He shrugged and turned to stare out of the window.

"I haven't seen anything I haven't told you about. We're all in this together and I am truly grateful to you." I noticed that, although they were sitting side-by-side, Biro didn't talk to March for the next hour. And March didn't talk to Biro. He did try once, but Biro would not be drawn. There was an undercurrent of hostility which was uncomfortable. It permeated the car.

"What about you, Biro? How do things feel to you?"

He shrugged. "I dunno . . . it's just . . . never mind. Some other time."

"OK."

Stress, conflict, tension were, I mused, the stuff of drama. Where is the film without an inciting incident? A murder, a meeting, a burglary. Well, my burglary was the inciting incident for this memoir. You set out with an issue or an act that needs resolving during the course of the film or novel and you do it. We were right in the midst of resolving our particular issue and we didn't need an internal struggle. It occurred to me that maybe Biro was put out. He had been the number one man after me. Had his role changed? Or had his cage just been rattled somewhat? I would have to wait and see.

Chapter Eighteen

ROADSIDE ASSISTANCE

"Priority rescue for anyone in a *vulnerable* situation."
RAC

I drove for the rest of that afternoon. North. It was going to be a five-hour drive. I took the A835 in the direction of Ullapool then tried a short cut across the hills on a tiny road when the unexpected happened. Without any forewarning the car slowed to a stop. Biro had been snoozing. He woke with a start, "We outta gas?"

I glanced down at the gauge. "No. We're still holding on half a tank."

Susie looked around at the landscape. "Wow, John. She couldn't have chosen a more remote spot to quit."

I tried starting the car several times. No go. I couldn't see any untoward glowing lights on the display.

Susie got out of the car. We all did.

"I don't suppose it would be any good us looking under the bonnet?" I asked no one in particular. Biro shrugged. Susie ignored me. "I thought not. So . . . we don't have membership with any roadside rescue service. I just didn't think a brand new Mercedes would break down."

I got out my new phone and managed to connect with google. I took down the numbers of a couple of garages in Inverness and called them.

The second I called knew something about Mercedes and they could come out to tow us in straight away. I described as best I could to them where we were. I had the road numbers, etc. off the sat nav.

Susie was quiet, sitting off to the side on a rock. "You, OK?"

"Yes, John. Fine. Thank you. I was in a mathematical problem I have on at the moment. It's a real brain-teaser, but that's how I like 'em. Difficult."

"No point telling me, I guess.

"No. No point, John. Sorry."

"Just say what it is and see if it means anything."

"It won't mean anything. But it doesn't matter . . . I was thinking about the work of two mathematicians called Tomio Kubota and Heinrich-Wolfgang Leopoldt. They used Kummer's congruences for Bernoulli numbers to construct a p-adic L-function, the p-adic Riemann zeta function . . . Are you with me, John?"

I laughed. "OK. Susie. I take your point. But sometime please tell me something I could grasp. I'd like to try to understand better why you find numbers so exciting."

"I will . . . try . . . sometime"

Biro came up to me, "I just want you to know, John, that things have really improved for me since I joined up with you."

"That's good to hear, my friend. I shan't forget it."

We had to wait an hour, but the breakdown truck did eventually arrive and two men in blue overalls jumped out. One of them was a large man and the other small and skinny. Serious echoes of Nothing and Everywhere, which was spooky.

Amazingly the small one recognised Biro immediately. "Hello again."

It was so unexpected and very weird—out here in this remote spot with hardly a farm in sight and no other cars. Biro was taken aback, but managed to say, "Sorry. I don't recall meeting you. Sure you've got the right person?"

"It's Biro, isn't it?" the small one retorted. He reminded me of an ingrown toenail. He was sort of bent in on himself and somewhat discoloured.

Biro kept up his blank look.

"It was on the midwest tour with Buckle Down. I was on that crew too."

Biro smiled slowly, realising he had to admit that he knew him. "Yes. I've got it. I remember that tour—just!" He slapped Ingrown on the back. "Good to see you again."

"Likewise. What're you lot doing up here?"

"We're just on our way to visit friends near Ullapool," I cut in.

The big engineer tried to start the car. He shook his head at me as he moved back to the truck. "We will have to tow her in. We don't have the equipment with us to attempt repairs here." He had a broad Scottish accent, unlike Ingrown, who sounded distinctly south London.

"Whatcha been doin' since the US tour?"

"Oh, bit of this and that. How 'bout you, Doplock?"

"I bin up here a few years now. Came for a change, then a friend heard about this job . . . and here I am."

The big engineer drove the truck to the front of the car. Ingrown started to unhitch the tow chain and run it out. Biro looked concerned and whispered to me, "I feel strange about this. D'you think it's odd?"

"What?"

"Him turning up and all and recognising me. Does it . . . mean anything?"

"It's odd, I grant you, and a little disconcerting. But . . ."

"Yes, John?"

"I don't think it means anything, Biro, other than what it appears on the surface."

Susie was still reading on the rock. I sat next to her. "Well, I guess this means at least a night in Inverness. Ever been there?"

She shook her head. "Fine by me. I'm just along for the ride."

I hoped it was more than this, but didn't know what to say, so I let it go.

When the car was hitched up and linked, we all climbed into the back seat of the truck. It was cramped. I was sitting between March and Susie. It was cosy and, under the circumstances, I enjoyed the ride. The big engineer said he would put the car straight into the repair bay and try to order any spares by close of business so it could be fixed tomorrow and we could be on our way the following night. We gave him our full support and watched the beautiful scenery flow by. A big old 50s Buick passed us going in the opposite direction. It was an incongruous sight in that setting

March watched the car intently over his shoulder until it was out of sight. "Reminds me of Cuba."

"What does, March?"

"That big old Buick, John." He was silent for a minute then went on. "Spent a year in Havana researching a novel. Never wrote it. Still intend to though . . . one day. That city was somethin' else—the architecture, the colour, the dominance on the streets of those 50s limos. Like nowhere else in the world. It buzzed and got right under my skin. But I ran up hard against the government and they threw me out. Didn't even let me get my case from the hotel. Put me straight on a plane for Paris, which was OK in the end because I'd never been there." He stared out the truck window for a few minutes. "I was disappointed about Cuba. I had hoped to do something useful there—for the Cuban people, I mean, not for the US government."

Susie laughed, "I knew what you meant, uncle. You've always tried to do something useful. We all know that."

"Useful for people?"

"No, for our family I mean."

"Oh, them . . . well. I think by now they've completely forgotten me."

"You should keep in touch, March."

"No point. We live on different sides of the fence. And, anyway, here you are, Susie. I am in touch."

"Only with me."

"And that, dear Susie, is more than enough for me." He chuckled.

"What's that supposed to mean?"

"Just that. I am in touch with you and that's enough family for me."

"Well, thank you, March. I guess I must take than as a compliment."

"It is. You're one in a million."

I looked at Susie, "I second that. Can't have too many brilliant people in one family." I glanced at March. He seemed to like this, but Susie just dismissed it with a shrug and no comment.

Ingrown squirmed round in his seat, "So where d'you live now, Biro?"

Biro wasn't keen to talk. "North London."

"Got a flat?"

"Sort of."

"Sort of, Biro?"

Yes, sort of."

"Well, either you 'ave or you 'aven't."

"Look, it's not a cut and dried issue. OK. It's in flux."

"Why's that, Biro?"

"Just is."

Biro was looking uncomfortable so I butted in, "We're going to buy a house together, do it up and then sell. We need to make some money."

"This car looks like money to me," Ingrown laughed.

"May look like it but it's not ours. Leased."

"Nice work if you can get." He turned away from us.

I shrugged.

Chapter Nineteen

THE REGIMENT

Per Ardua ad Astra

We went shopping in the morning and found a camera store where I bought three more pairs of binoculars. At a nearby chemist I picked up a box of rubber gloves and a couple of ordnance survey maps at a bookshop.

The call that the car was ready came just after 4:00pm. We took a cab to the garage. The Merc looked and sounded great. The engine was purring nicely and they had cleaned her inside and out. Nice service.

While we waited for the bill Ingrown sidled up to Biro. "Went on facebook last night and found a friend of yours we both know. Gus Oldenburg."

"Not his real name. We called him that after our posting at RAF Oldenburg. We were there before The Regiment went over to Basrah."

My ears pricked up. "You in the SAS, Biro?"

Susie came closer to listen.

"Nah. RAF Regiment."

"Never heard of it, Biro."

"Why should you? It's no big deal, John."

"But you in the military does come as a big surprise."

"Why, John? We all have to do something . . ."

"I wouldn't have put you down as a soldier."

"Why not?"

"Don't know exactly. Just . . ."

Ingrown picked up the pause, "Gus says you were his Sarge."

"Yes, well, that is true, man. Can't deny it."

"Wow, Biro! A true leader of men. Don't they say that sergeants run the army?"

"They do indeed, John. And we did. The junior ruperts were a dead loss and more trouble than they were worth."

"Gus said that after your cushy posting in Oldenburg your next tour was in Basrah. Guess that wasn't a picnic."

"You could say."

"D'you see any combat, Biro?"

"Oh, come on, Doplock. What d'you wanna hear? Some gruesome war story? Want some vicarious pleasure, do you?"

"Come again."

"Wanna know if I was scared in firefights or that I shot someone—something like that?"

"Well, did you, Biro?"

"What?"

"Shoot anyone?"

"I knew it! Sick."

I couldn't help myself chiming in too, "Did you, Biro?"

"It was part of the job. OK?"

"Yes, but did you?" Susie asked.

"I did."

"Did you kill 'em?" squeaked Ingrown.

"Oh, boy," sighed Biro. "It's not something I care to remember."

We were all waiting for an answer but Biro walked away. Ingrown shrugged and I paid the bill.

We drove out of town and for over 10 miles in silence. Biro just stared out the window. To break the silence I asked Susie if she would like to drive. She nodded. We stopped and changed seats.

Biro decided it was time to speak. "Fact is there's nothing like being in a firefight and surviving. Best feeling in the world. Time stands still and the fear just drains away. When the bullets are whipping and pinging round your head you rise up, take 'em and fire back. Get some! The point being to kill them before they kill you. It is exciting, the most exciting thing ever: better'n drugs, better'n sex, but it's also fucking awful when you come down and see the carnage—broken bodies, friends, pals dead. The pain, the screaming the suffering . . . D'you know who dying soldiers ask for help?"

"God?"

"Sometimes, yes, John, but mostly they call out for their mothers."

"What goes around comes around," commented Susie. She wasn't being cynical.

"I did kill once. Young Iraqi soldier. Very young. He shouldn't have been there. It was not my fault, but I still feel guilt. Guess I always will."

We cruised on in silence. I wanted to say something, but decided to bide my time.

"Next day we were in combat again and this time I was hit in the chest. Slotted good and proper. Felt like someone had punched me real hard. The bullet had gone right through me. The entry wound was small, bullet-sized. The exit wound was bigger. "'Bout the size of a cricket ball. Know what the US grunts used to say in Iraq?"

We waited.

"Payback is a mother-fucker."

Chapter Twenty

SNAKES IN THE GRASS

"The serpent beguiled me, and I did eat."
Genesis Chapter 3, verse 13.

I asked Susie to take a side road. After a mile we passed a grove of magnificent, ancient oaks standing in a rocky glade. Susie pulled over and we went our separate ways to find a quiet spot. I walked through the glade. The huge oaks were covered in thick vibrant green moss. They looked like miniature forest-clad mountains. The oaks were also covered with moss. It had a magical, timeless feel about it and reminded me of acid trips in days gone by.

I took over the wheel again after the stop. The further we drove, though, the more ill at ease I became. The fact that Ingrown recognized Biro had concerned me. I was becoming more and more suspicious as time went on. The nagging feeling that we were being followed kept growing even though I never saw anything in the rearview mirror to seriously support my paranoia.

We were on the A87, heading for the Kyle of Lochalsh when I spotted a nondescript green car, which stayed behind us at about the same distance for five or six miles. I pulled into the side of the road at the next lay-by. I said I needed to pee. A few seconds after we'd stopped the green car drove by and carried on up the road. I didn't recognize the driver. His face was turned away from me. A big man certainly. It could well have been Everywhere. I was the only one who took any notice of the passing car. The others were not in the slightest bit interested but I had been the only one with a rearview mirror. I was surprised Biro had not picked up on it. To ease the strain I asked Susie to drive again. I checked either side of the road as we cruised along—side turnings, gateways and drives, but didn't see that car again.

"D'you know what?" I turned to Susie. She glanced over at me. She looked so good behind the wheel.

"I feel a lot safer now I know that we have a salty sarge along with us. Someone who's used to a bit of a drama and putting up a fight." I looked back over my shoulder, "I thought I was onto a good thing when I teamed up with you, Biro. Very comforting."

He smiled, almost laughed. It started to rain and went on for an hour.

"What is this RAF Regiment thing all about, Biro?" It was the first thing March had said in a long while.

"It's the infantry group attached to the RAF."

"To do what?"

"Guard the aircraft, stores, personnel and mainly the airfield perimeters. Just that. We had Puma helicopters in Baghdad, which assisted the Foreign and Commonwealth Office. We had Merlin choppers to assist with the withdrawal of equipment and personnel and some Harriers. We had a few C130 Hercules aircraft too to provide transport in and out of the country."

"Don't have anything like that in the US of A as far as I know," March responded.

"You have your marines for that," Biro replied."

"They're not my marines, son. Not my USA either, come to that."

I put in my three ha'pence worth, "So why d'you join this regiment and not the regular army, Biro?"

"They told us that it was an elite unit, that we'd get specialist training. Blah, blah . . ."

"And was it?"

"Bollocks it was! The guys in The Regiment liked to believe it and then project that elite image. But they're not elite. Not at all. Just ordinary grunts who joined up to impress and swell their egos. It was all very disappointing."

By the time we approached Loch Broom the rain had stopped and the sun had come out, albeit low in the sky. We drove alongside the Loch in the twilight. It was staggeringly beautiful. The water was a perfect mirror, steely and still. Susie parked in a lay-by and we all left the car to take in the view.

"This sure is something, ain't it?" March asked no one in particular. He walked off alone along the side of the Loch. The three of us sat down beside the Merc.

Susie spoke first, "Getting close now, John. How d'you feel?"

"Nervous. How 'bout you?"

"Nervous, but I like it. We're a motley crew and I like that too. This whole thing is . . . intriguing and kinda quirky."

"You could say, Susie."

Just then the green car, which had been behind us earlier, went by in the opposite direction. Again the driver had his face averted as he closed with us and passed on by. I looked at the others. Cool as cucumbers and blissfully unaware. I kept quiet. There was no need to stir the pot at this delicate stage.

I walked over to Biro and drew him off a short distance to the shore of the Loch. "That stuff you told us about the RAF Regiment got me thinking."

"I thought it would." He laughed.

"I'm getting cold feet about the guns."

"Oh, yeah? Why's that?"

"Apart from the fact that I'm a peace-loving vegetarian, we could drop ourselves into some deep shit if we actually use 'em and hit someone . . . or worse . . ."

"Leave it to me, John. I'll take the first shot. I know how to aim at people and miss. Used to do it all the time."

"Is that right?"

"Whatever people say it's not easy to fire a bullet at someone you don't know and aren't personally angry with. A lot of the time soldiers in combat are known to shoot high. They just can't bring themselves to take life."

"I had no idea."

"I guess it's not common knowledge, John."

"I can see it wouldn't do much for morale or for boosting aggression."

"You got it." He was silent for a couple of minutes. We looked out across the Loch enjoying its tranquility. "We just had to look on it as a job, John—something we'd been hired for and paid for and something we were committed to do." We walked on along the shore. "When I'd been patched up and all my bits were working right again I quit The Regiment. Really I wasn't fit enough mentally or physically to go back on the line."

"Were you pleased?"

"Yes, in a kinda way. Though I missed the camaraderie and being part of a team. We could—and did—rely on one another. We were all on the edge together. The same chaotic edge."

"So this . . . er . . . jaunt appealed to your . . . spirit of adventure?"

"Oh, yes, John. And you can count on me one hundred percent."

"And you don't mind the guns, Biro?"

"I'm at home around guns. Always have been."

"What is it you like about them?"

Biro thought for a minute. "It's that cracking sound. It splits the air, ripping it open. Nothing can get to you like the sound of gunfire—'specially an automatic weapon like an AK. Pop, pop, pop. It's exhilarating, John. It really is—'specially if the gun is aimed at you. You can hear the bullets pass you by with a kind of whoosh and fizz. Of course if you can hear 'em you're OK. They've missed. Nothing gets your attention like that. Surviving a firefight. What a buzz, my dear fellow!"

"So will you handle the guns if it comes to it and we need to . . . use 'em?"

"Sure. I'll do it if you really can't."

I looked out over the Loch. All this talk about firefights and combat had got me thinking. Deep down I guess I had always hankered after the experience of war, of fighting. What I wanted to know was if I would have the courage to face up to the fight or if I would crumble into a blubbering heap of nerves. I wanted to be tested and I wanted to prove I had it in me to survive the test however terrifying it turned out to be. So, I concluded, maybe this was to be my opportunity—my baptism—and I really had to go through with it.

We turned and walked back towards the car. We could see Susie and March standing close together, talking.

"Not a one of us joined The Regiment because we wanted to kill someone, John. That wasn't the point. Grunts on the whole are not sadists, but they do love the adventure and the camaraderie. No question."

I thought for a while. "What about March? How does he fit in?"

"I don't think he does, but he might come in useful in some way . . . watching our backs."

"He seems pretty gung-ho."

"Yeah, and that could be a problem."

"How, Biro?"

"If he doesn't do as he's told or starts to lose it."

"Is that likely?"

"You never know, man. You never know. Keep your powder dry."

As we neared the car we could see that March and Susie were deep in conversation and not aware of our approach. I heard March ask, "But what are you doing with him, Susie? He's OK, but you . . ." Then he caught sight of me and didn't finish what he was saying but I guessed it might have been something like "could do better."

I felt this too. She was a pearl and I was a swine. I was a very ordinary man in the light of her sparkling brilliance, no question. It was puzzling. Why was she with us? Was it because of me? If it was, the question I asked myself was: what does she see in me? It made more sense in a way if she wasn't here because of me but for the ride, the excitement, the mystery. Ah, well, I thought, all will be revealed in the fullness of time. Amen.

Susie smiled at me in a kindly way as Biro and I reached the car. It was reassuring and I felt my spirits lift.

"Let's get on to Ullapool. OK? I started towards the driver's door then turned to look back. "You want to drive, Susie?"

"No, you do it. I'll sit in the back with March."

This unnerved me again. I didn't want them to get too close. I didn't want to be left out. I very easily fell foul of that most pernicious emotion called jealousy. It could eat a man up then spit him out like a dried old prune. We climbed into the car and I drove off.

Biro turned to me, "Sometime soon we better break out those weapons so I can check 'em over."

I nodded. "Sure. Let's do it tonight."

Biro signed off with, "And, everyone, *don't forget* to charge your phones."

Chapter Twenty One

THE QUEEN OF HEARTS

**"The Queen of Hearts she made some tarts all on a
summer's day;
The Knave of Hearts he stole the tarts and
took them clean away."
Lewis Carroll.
Alice in Wonderland**

Biro tracked down a reasonable hotel in Ullapool and checked
us in under my Wheat Trailer name open-ended. As we drove
into town Susie said right out of the blue, "I really must teach
you some math, John. I have a feeling you'd get something out
of it."

I looked at her and smiled. "Take your word for it, Susie."

Turning into the hotel car park I caught sight of a figure
dressed in a long, black waterproof coat and sou'wester hat.
There was something about him that seemed very out of place
even in this setting. For one thing he was obviously over-dressed.
It was only drizzling slightly, more like a heavy mist, though when
one becomes the other and vice versa is hard to say. I didn't quite

see his face but the way he hung his arms looked familiar. I didn't mention him to the other three straightaway. A small voice was telling me though that I should at the very least speak to Biro about it. After we had arrived and checked in Biro and March made a beeline for the bar. I turned down the offer to join them. Susie and I went upstairs.

All our rooms looked out over open country. The sun had scraped through the clouds and was dancing over the wild green and brown landscape. The trees were bending to the wind.

I thought about what Susie had said just now about teaching me some maths. I wondered if she had been teasing me or if she meant it. And if she meant it, what did she hope to teach me. I could add and subtract, multiply and divide. I knew my times-tables and I could do percentages. I felt I had all the maths I needed. I thought I had a grip on geometry and could just about see the point of algebra.

The sky cleared abruptly. It was a pure, deep blue. It cheered me up, gave me the confidence to call on Susie. Her room was two doors away. I knocked, pressing my ear to the door. I heard her cross the room.

"Who's there?"

"John."

"Hold on." She unlocked the door and opened it to let me in. I could see she'd been working.

"I hope I'm not disturbing you, Susie."

"It's OK. I was reading a math paper."

"What's it on?" I asked innocently.

"D'you really want to know?"

"Yes." I laughed. I was nervous.

"Sure about that?"

"Yes. Absolutely."

"It's about the Kenkichi Iwasawa theory."

"Jeez! And what's that?"

"The philosophy that special values of L-functions contain arithmetic information." Susie shrugged and turned back to her laptop.

I walked over to her and, looking over her shoulder, I read: "The Galois group of the infinite tower, the starting field, and the sort of arithmetic module studied can all be varied. In each case there is a main conjecture linking the tower to a p-adic L-function."

She looked up at me. "You see?"

"Yes, I see . . . or don't see, not really."

"It's just a language, John. Like learning any language,"

"Yes, OK . . . but what's it all for? What d'you *do* with it?"

"You do numbers with it, John."

"And then what?"

"That's it. It's pure mathematics, You don't *do* anything with it. The numbers reveal a beautiful and wonderful world. You find order, meaning. It's an end in itself."

"You make it sound . . . intriguing and mysterious. Exciting even."

"I do it because it's there, John . . . and, yes, it is exciting. The great mathematician G H Hardy once wrote: mathematics is of all the arts and sciences the most remote."

She looked back at what she'd been reading. She closed the file and opened another application. She typed in some instructions, pressed enter. There was a pause and the screen lit up with an image of a black, spikey blob, surrounded by pulsating coloured waves, forming into branching tree-like structures, curlicues and shapes that looked like elephant trunks, sea-horses, compound insect eyes and paisley patterns. The black shape resembled an insect combined with a hairy potato. It also looked like a man. It looked like a cat, an insect or a cactus. Susie pressed enter again and the image zoomed into the spike at the head-like end of the black shape. The zoom continued deep into the spike. The colours cycled through multiple rainbow hues and the patterns evolved, but always on a theme. The first thought that dashed into my mind was: LSD. I recognised these patterns. These were the colours and the shapes I had seen and been a part of at the height of a trip. I decided to keep this observation under wraps until I knew a lot more about Susie and could sense how she would react to this side of my life. I put my hands onto her shoulders and leaned in closer to the screen. Susie pressed a key, the zoom froze and the image reverted to the original black shape. "What is this?"

"It's called the Mandelbrot set."

"The what?"

Susie laughed and her shoulders shook. She looked up at me and smiled. I felt my knees go weak again and my pulse picked up. I wondered if she could feel the heat coming through my hands. "It's the Mandelbrot set. Oddly enough Mandelbrot in German means almond-bread. That always strikes me as funny. Dunno why. It's not significant."

I managed to pull myself together and find my voice. "So what is this Mandelbrot set?"

"It's an infinitely complex mathematical entity, which was discovered—found—by Benoît Mandelbrot on March 1st 1980."

"On one day?"

"Yes, on that very day. The thing is that the set couldn't have been discovered before the era of modern computers. Mandelbrot was a mathematician, who was working at IBM on the development of a branch of mathematics he later called fractal geometry. IBM had some of the most powerful machines in the world at that time. Mandelbrot and his team were working on visualising things called Julia sets." She typed in some instructions. The screen cleared and then revealed a series of colourful whirling patterns. I could see in the shapes that the patterns were being repeated over smaller and smaller scales. It reminded me of a fern, where small leaves grow off bigger leaves, repeating the same basic shape.

These are Julia sets and there are infinite number of them. "The Mandelbrot set is in fact a dictionary of all the Julia sets. It contains them all within itself."

"This is a mighty strange world, Susie. It all seems to have some meaning and maybe have something to do with real life. I mean apart from the beautiful images."

"Yes, well, the images do certainly remind us of things we see in the real world. That's well established."

I caught site of the clock in the bottom right hand corner of her screen. "It's later than I thought, Susie. I promised to . . . do that thing with Biro . . ."

"Ah, yes . . . well, you'd better do it then, John.

Chapter Twenty Two

ARE BULLETS PHALLIC?

**"Making and selling Sugar Gliders—fragmenting
bullets—is definitely not OK.
What kind of a person would do a thing like that?"
Norman Mailer**

There's something very exciting to me about women who do
science and that certainly applies to mathematics. It's just the
same for me with girls who fly fast jets or combat helicopters.
Smart, successful business women in sharp suits don't do it for
me. It's only half there with doctors and nurses.

I knocked on Biro's door and waited. It cracked open and
Biro peaked through. "OK, John. Come in." He closed the door
quickly and quietly. I walked in the room. The bed was covered
in carefully laid out gun parts. Biro had a white cloth and a small
oilcan in his hand.

"They're both in pretty good shape. Neither is very worn.
There's some slackness in the return spring in the Beretta, but
it's good for many more rounds yet. I tightened the pinion.

They're all greased up so watch me reassemble them so you can see what they're made of."

I watched him in silence.

Biro worked quickly. He clearly knew what he was doing. All the elements fitted together with resounding clunks and clicks. He looked satisfied when he handed the Sig-Sauer to me.

"See that switch at the top of the grip, John? That's your safety. On or off. It's essential, but couldn't be simpler."

I nodded, turning the gun over in my hand.

"Always hold the gun with both hands and when you fire, fire low. The gun will buck and the shot will go high." He leaned back on the bed and reached for a shallow box. The three magazines were inside. Biro picked up one of the Sig-Sauer magazines and flicked out one round, which he held in his hand in front of me. "Lethal, but somehow strangely beautiful." He passed the bullet to me. "What d'you think of it?"

"It's heavy. It's clean, shiny. Nice shape."

"What does that shape remind you of, John?"

I weighed it in my hands. "Well, I guess it's phallic. Looks like a willy."

"Does, doesn't it? Like some universal form."

"You're starting to sound like Susie, Biro."

"Huh?"

"Susie and her mathematics. She's been showing me some amazing stuff on her laptop."

"Only on her laptop!"

I blushed and looked down at the bullet in my hand.

"It's pretty obvious you're completely gone on her, John. And I don't blame you."

"Does she like me, Biro?" I asked with too much enthusiasm.

"Course, she does, John."

"Really?"

"Yes."

"Oh, boy." I couldn't hide my feelings but I trusted Biro. I knew by then that he was a loyal friend and that I could risk it.

"Just take your time, John. Don't rush it. Let it grow gently."

I handed the bullet back to Biro.

He went back to the business in hand. "To recap then. We have 39 rounds between us with one spare mag for the Sig."

"Well, you have 39 rounds."

"No, John. We go in with a gun each. I'll take the Beretta. You take the Sig."

"I can't shoot at anyone. I just can't do that."

"If it comes to it—and I hope it won't—and you do have to fire, you are almost certain to miss."

"How come?"

"You've had no practice, John. You've not tried firing it. Put it this way, if you do fire it and hit someone it would be a complete bloody fluke."

"You're kidding me, Biro."

"No, I'm not. They make it look easy in the movies, but it isn't. It takes a lot of practice. You might turn out to be a very fine shot, John, with a bit of preparation. Only now you won't be. So don't worry."

I laughed at the incongruity of the situation.

"Thing is it'll look so much more intimidating if we both go in armed. You can see that I'm sure. So, agreed?"

"Yeah, agreed, Biro."

"I'll put these away. You better get back to your maths class." He winked.

I watched him place the guns gently into a small rucksack, which he put in the bottom of his holdall.

"Good night, John.

"G'night, Biro."

Chapter Twenty Three

THE MANDELBROT SET

**'The most beautiful thing we can
experience is the mysterious.
It is the source of all true art and science.'
Albert Einstein**

I tapped cautiously on Susie's door.

"Come in."

It was unlocked. I went in. Susie was still at the desk with her laptop. She gestured for me join her by the machine. I looked over her shoulder and read:

In *mathematics*, a *p*-adic zeta function, or more generally a *p*-adic *L*-function, is a function analogous to the *Riemann zeta function*, or more general *L-functions*, but whose *domain* and *target* are *p-adic* (where *p* is a *prime number*). I turned away from the screen, feeling dizzy. Susie laughed and closed the file. Once more the Mandelbrot set appeared on the screen.

"You know Albert Einstein's famous theory?" She turned to me as she finished the question.

"Sure. E equals m c squared."

"And you get what it means?"

"Basically."

"It's a powerful equation, but a very simple one too."

"It impresses me that so much power can come out of apparently so little."

Susie glanced back at the screen, "Well, the equation for the Mandelbrot set is equally simple, z equals z squared plus c. You allocate numbers to the letters and do the sum. There are a couple of other extra elements in this formula though. First thing is the equals sign is actually a double arrow. The numbers flow in both directions, constantly feeding back on themselves. It's like a dog chasing its own tail. The output of one operation becomes the input of the next, becomes the output . . . and so on, round and round. The process is called iteration. If you can do this sum millions, billions of times you can generate the Mandelbrot set. And that's why it wasn't discovered until the arrival of computers." She looked up at me. "Are you with me still?"

I nodded. I could follow her this far.

"OK. The other thing about the equation is the very weird and wonderful element tacked under the letter c. And it is 'i', which is the square root of minus one. It's what's known as a complex number."

She waited for a reaction. I walked round to stand more in front of her and took her hand. It was delicate and warm. Very soft. She turned hers over so our palms were touching and squeezed my hand just a little.

"Complex numbers, John, are among the most important ideas in the whole of mathematics. They have their own arithmetic, algebra and so on. They rely for their existence on pure mathematical imagination: the square root of minus one."

I must have looked completely lost.

"Would you like to hear more about this stuff or am I boring you? Shall we leave it there?"

"No. I like it. I do really." To be honest she could have told me anything she liked. I was putty in her hands. She stood and went to sit on the bed. I walked with her and sat beside her.

"I'll give you a bit of background and history then. Since the square root of a negative number cannot be placed anywhere on the number line, mathematicians up to the C19th couldn't ascribe anything real to them. The great Wilhelm Leibnitz, who invented the Differential Calculus, attributed a mystical quality to 0, seeing it as a manifestation of a divine spirit. He called it 'that amphibian between being and not being'. How ''bout that?''

"It certainly has a kinda mystical feel about it. I get that, Susie. There is something biblical about it too. Like Genesis—the creation of the world."

It was turning out that this maths rang bells for me. I guessed I really had found something new I liked. I was inspired. I suddenly saw whole new vistas opening up for me. "As I see it then these complex numbers somehow only exist in the mind. Is that how you see it?"

"Exactly. Of course that's how I see it, John. These numbers are not found out here in the physical world. As you say, they only exist in minds . . . and now in computers of course."

I didn't say anything. I was waiting for more.

"A century after Leibnitz Leonhard Euler wrote that all expressions such as the square root of minus one are impossible or imaginary numbers, since they represent roots of negative quantities. Of such numbers we may truly assert that they are neither nothing, nor greater than nothing, nor less than nothing. Eventually a mathematician called Carl Gauss proposed that an objective existence can be assigned to these imaginary beings. He saw that there was no room for imaginary numbers anywhere on the real number line, which runs from east to west. So what he did was to take the really bold step of placing these numbers on a perpendicular axis, running north to south. He created a new co-ordinate system. All the real numbers are placed on the 'real axis' and all the imaginary numbers on the 'imaginary axis'. Cool?"

"Yup."

She stroked my hand and lifted her face to me. She was so pretty. I hardly dared to kiss her, but I did and it worked wonders for both of us. Her lips were soft and silky. Her cheeks as well. She held me. I wanted to gasp. This was a miracle. There is a God, I thought! I kissed her ears and her hair. That delicious smell of new-mown hay again. She lay back on the bed, taking off her blouse . . .

. . . I won't attempt to describe what happened after that. It was frankly beyond my powers of description. And, anyway, it would be prurient and indulgent. This is not a damn Mills and Boon. No *Gold Angel* by Stainless Steele!

But I'll say this: for us, it was a great thing. We slept that night together. My dreams were like flying. Numbers and Susie.

When I woke the next morning I looked at Susie lying beside me. She was still asleep. She looked so beautiful. I wondered if maybe I was in the presence of an angel. A wave of fear rolled over me and then I remembered the story of Guru Arjun Dev, the 5th Sikh Guru and I resolved to hang tough. History tells us that he was imprisoned and excessively tortured for his faith. His body was exposed in the scorching heat of the May-June sun. He was made to sit on the red-hot sand, and boiling hot water was poured on his naked body before he finally gave up the ghost. My guru referred to him as a very bold saint. Wow! You could say. It put my fear in perspective.

Chapter Twenty Four

BUSMAN AND A RIPPLE OF CONFLICT

"He's got the whole world in his hands."
Unknown

Susie and I went into the dining room together. I put Guru Arjun Dev out of my mind as we joined Biro and March for breakfast. The fact that we were together didn't go unnoticed by the other two. We ordered. The two men were trying to find their feet. Susie and I were relaxed. We were floating along nicely.

Biro glanced at me. "I guess we're going to find the house and recce it today. Yes, John?"

"Yes, we are. You up for it, March?"

"Ready and willing." He glanced from me to Susie. "Did you get some math last night, John?" He asked innocently enough.

"Ah yes, a little. I got to see the Mandelbrot set and heard about complex numbers, we . . ."

March shrugged. "Lost me there, John. Never mind."

To change the subject I opened the local area ordnance survey map I'd bought and folded it to just the relevant area. I pointed to the spot on the map where I had worked out the house Drumrunnie should be. There was a track from the road to the coast, which was about half a mile long. It appeared to run right past Drumrunnie.

Biro took the map and studied it. He looked up. "I think it best we find a lockup for the Merc and rent something else. That car does stand out a bit."

I took his point. Breakfast started to arrive. We stopped talking for a few minutes. Next to us four elderly folk were also eating. One of them was holding court. He was a big man with a shiny bald head and a loud voice. "If you can pick up the 313 at Inhampton you can catch the Taylor-Greenswell X40 at Invergarry bus station just before five. It's a good service. I remember once when it was cancelled and we had to take the Green Line up to the museum and wait there for the 29, which is OK if the A90's clear."

I glanced at Biro. He was shaking his head and barely suppressing a laugh. When he caught my eye the flood gates opened and he spluttered out loud. Susie and March were giggling. Busman didn't notice. He just ploughed on. His companions seemed totally gripped by his knowledge and listened with their full attention. None of them seemed to notice our hysterics at the next table.

"They're comfortable coaches and sometimes there's a toilet even. On Thursdays the Getabus service run an extra mid-morning coach, but it goes all round the houses and often gets cancelled. When it works, it's great 'cause it links up with the 118 outside the Apollo and that misses out the slow run down the B349. It's a single-decker though so you don't get a good view."

We were nearly falling off our chairs, rocking with laughter, but on he went.

"The best ride I ever had was down in Exeter on the Smart-Wilkins 109. Amazing. It links with the 204 and with the Hope 12. On a Thursday it'll take you as far as the terminus in time to pick up the last running of the 63".

Spluttering, Biro broke our silence, "I'm gonna set up a car rental and I want to check out where we can hire a seaworthy boat at short notice. We'll need to go on a short jaunt along the coast and out to sea a bit when the job is done and if certain things happen." He managed to choke back his giggles and attempted to look serious. I wiped my eyes and tried to ignore the bald-headed ranter.

I managed to focus on Biro's suggestion. I wasn't put out by the idea. I thought it sounded good. Why it might be necessary wasn't completely clear to me. But that didn't matter because Biro always seemed to have thought things through and to know what he was doing. "Do that, please, Biro. Let me know how much."

Busman pressed on. "The first time I took the 42 from Victoria Coach Station it broke down on the A6 and we didn't get a replacement for over two hours. They gave us vouchers though."

Biro stumbled to his feet. He was squeaking, trying not to laugh. He left the room. I couldn't finish my breakfast. Susie took my hand under the table and squeezed it. March was going purple in the face, holding back hysterics. He jumped to his feet, looked at Busman and stumbled from the room. His shoulders were shaking.

We had more coffee. Busman kept on rambling. The smaller of the two women suddenly piped up, "The 36 is a much better bus, better route . . ." Her words faded away as Busman gave her a withering look and then pressed on again. It was starting to get boring and I hoped Biro would be finished soon. A few minutes later his head appeared around the door to the dining room and he beckoned me over. I went outside with him. Slanting rain blasted into the hotel entrance. We sheltered out of the wind.

"I fixed up a car for us—an SUV in case we need all four wheels. We can pick it up in an hour. I've arranged with the owner of some lockups to meet us in his yard at noon. And I've found a sea-going launch we can put on standby for two days and two nights for 500. I said we'd drop off the cash tonight. OK?"

"OK, Biro. You never cease to impress me."

"It's just what I do, John, my boy."

I clapped him on the back. We looked out into the rain.

"We used to call it the 7 Ps in The Regiment." He looked round at me, "Proper planning and preparation prevent piss-poor performance." He smiled. "Usually works."

We went first to a camping store and bought groundsheets, sleeping bags, wet weather gear, a gas stove, several gas cylinders, four vacuum flasks, a kettle and two Swiss army knives—the big ones.

The guy was waiting for us at the lockup when we got there. We transferred our stuff from the Merc and put it in the SUV. I paid him the cash for a week in advance. It seemed to cheer him up. We clambered in and set off. The rain continued to beat down. I drove carefully through the deep puddles and the low visibility. It was a very comfortable drive though. I sort of preferred it to the Merc, which surprised me. We stopped at a big supermarket on the edge of the town and picked up enough provisions for three days—a lot of water and plenty of dried fruit.

I told Susie and March about putting the launch on standby in case we did have to lose something in the sea after the push. All the while I kept my eyes open, constantly scanning all around. I couldn't see much out of the rear window. I had to keep the wipers on continuously. I noticed that Biro and Susie were both very alert.

On the narrow road out of Inverkirkaik we didn't say much for a few miles then from nowhere March launched off. "It really pisses me off when I hear people demanding their rights. There was a guy in front of me in the post office the other day demanding his rights over and over. What rights did he think he has? I don't have any rights. Nothing is mine. I don't—can't—really *own* anything. When I die I will say goodbye to the things I thought I owned and they'll be someone else's. And they probably won't even want 'em and they'll just drive 'em down to the dump. So I can't see that any one of us has any right to anything. We don't have entitlements to anything: like a weekly wage, like healthcare, like law and order, like a happy family. No one gets it all. No one *gets* anything. We are the property of the earth, and the earth is the property of the sun, and the sun is the property of the galaxy, and the galaxy is the property of the galactic super-cluster and the super-cluster is the property of the universe."

"You've got it all figured, then, March?"

"March shrugged, "Oh, I wouldn't say that, Biro. I'm just taking a stab at it."

Susie jumped in to support her uncle. "March wrote a book back in '97 called *The Property Fix*. It was kinda extreme, wouldn't you say, March?"

"It made people sit up and take notice, Susie—those few that read it. Caused a mini-stir. Got a coupla good reviews. Some bad ones too, of course. One guy said I was clinically insane and should be locked up, but he was from Arkansas: politics to the right of Genghis Khan."

March had got me thinking about human beings and their annoying foibles. When I'm writing I try my hardest to avoid clichés. That in itself sounds like a cliché as I write it. I can't stand phrases like 'at the end of the day', 'blue-sky thinking', 'no problem', quality time' and the crappiest of all 'thinking outside the box'. What sodding box?

My reverie was broken abruptly when I caught sight of black Sou'wester man. He was leaning on a five-bar gate, which was set back a couple of metres from the road. "Look!" All heads turned in the direction I was pointing. I slowed down. Sou'wester didn't hide his face. It was David Bowie.

"Holy shit! Are these people everywhere?" I realised the irony immediately I said it.

Susie shook her head.

"What the fuck is he doing here?" Biro joked but looked concerned.

"Who?" March was genuinely puzzled.

"David Bowie!" Susie looked intently at the passing figure.

"Who's David Bowie?" March persisted as we left Sou'wester fading into the mist.

"You can't be serious, March. David Bowie—the rock star." Biro was genuinely surprised.

"Nope."

"Well, it was a bit before my time, but haven't *you* heard of Space Oddity? You know, 'Ground Control to Major Tom; commencing count-down, engines on . . . 'All that"

"Nope. Heard of the Bowie Knife though. Colonel Jim Bowie used it in that famous duel called The Sandbar Fight."

"No, shit, March. But where've you been?" Biro was shaking his head in wonderment.

"Yes, Biro, but what about *him*?" I asked.

"Who? David Bowie?"

"No, Biro. The guy in the black coat and hat."

"Could've been anyone, but in the worst case, John, if he works for the target then we know that they know we're here. We have to face that possibility." Biro was thoughtful. "I saw him in the hotel car park last night too. Did you?"

"Yes, I did."

"Did you make anything of it then, John?"

"I dunno. I paused. "It was . . . sinister."

Susie looked from Biro to me. "Did he remind you of anyone, John?"

"Well, yes he did, Susie. Certainly. He stood like Everywhere and his arms hung in the same way."

"Then it's pretty definite that they know you're—we're—here."

"Yes it is, Susie."

"So does this make any difference to our plans?"

Biro jumped in, "What plans? Do we have a plan?"

I looked out across the hills and pondered. "OK. I would set it up like this. We park this beast and make it as invisible as possible. With our binoculars in hand we walk the last half mile, then find a good place where we can watch the house, but be hard for them to spot. Biro?"

"Yes, that's stage one. We're good for that, but as for stage two, I'm not sure. It'll depend on what we find. He leaned closer to the back of my seat. "And the guns, John? Do we take 'em?"

I pondered this too. Susie looked across at me, waiting. I shuddered and knew what we should do. "We take them, Biro."

Susie nodded and turned to the side window. March sighed loudly. I looked across at Biro in a kind of pleading way.

He turned to me and smiled. "Don't worry, John. Like I said, you'll miss."

We drove around the area, getting our bearings and a feel for the lay of the land. March didn't recall this particular spot. We checked all the surrounding roads and the location of nearby houses and farms. We found the side road that gave access to the path to the house and, where the road dipped, we chose a grove of oaks with space to get the SUV right off the road and in cover.

Satisfied that we had made some progress, we headed back to the hotel for some R 'n' R.

Chapter Twenty Five

DEAD ANGELS

"Take me on a trip upon your magic swirlin' ship.
My senses have been stripped,
my hands can't feel to grip,
My toes too numb to step, wait only for my boot heels
To be wanderin'.
I'm ready to go anywhere, I'm ready for to fade
Into my own parade, cast your dancing spell my way.
I promise to go under it."
Bob Dylan

After lunch Susie and I went to her room for a couple of hours. Then, feeling cheerful, we walked in the hills.

"D'you miss the USA?"

"No, not much . . . well, sometimes I do. Christmas, my birthday, Thanksgiving—times like that."

"When is your birthday, Susie?"

"February. February 6th."

"Aquarius."

"Oh, I wouldn't know about that, John."

"Not interested in astrology?"

"'Course not. It's bullshit."

"Is it?"

"Come on, John. Really?"

"But some people do seem to make sense of it."

"They make it up, John."

"Surely the positions of the planets must have some connection—some effect on us."

"Well, yes. Of course they have some connection with us."

"So, can't they influence us—influence our character at the time of our births?"

"No."

"But they're connected to us, Susie. You just said so."

"Yes, they are. But so are all the billions upon billions of stars in the entire fucking universe."

I had never heard her swear before and was taken aback. I gave her a sideways look. She waved her hand impatiently.

"You're an intelligent guy, John. You must be able to see through that nonsense."

"Well . . . yes. OK. I've never been completely hooked on it you'll be pleased to hear."

"I am."

We walked on hand in hand in silence for a while.

"When's your birthday, John?"

"6th November."

"Same day of the month as me. Is that significant?"

"Erm . . . I don't know, Susie."

"What sign's that?"

"Scorpio."

"Ah."

"What d'you mean by that?

"Like a scorpion, John."

"Am I?"

"Maybe."

"Why?"

She thought about this for a bit. "You seem to be—what shall I say?—a man of peace, a believer, and yet you appear to be prepared to use a gun to get back what is just a novel."

"Just a novel!"

"Yes. It's just words, John."

"Holy shit! It took me months to write."

"OK, John. But you could write it again and cut out all this risk, violence, danger."

"I couldn't. It just wouldn't be the same."

"Get a life, John. Be strong."

My anger took hold of me. "Fuck you." I stomped off across the rocky hillside, leaving Susie staring after me.

When I finally made it back to the hotel I was feeling dejected and remorseful. I almost crawled up to the door of Susie's room and knocked on the door. I heard her call out. "Who's there?"

I found I had lost my voice. I cleared my throat and gasped out, "It's me . . . John."

"Whaddya want?"

"I want to say sorry . . . apologise."

"Not now, John. Come back some other time."

I didn't know what to say. Full of guilt and pain, I slunk off with my tail, as they say, between my legs, went back to my room, took a shower and switched on the TV. I skimmed through the channels until I hit on a Wallander episode—thankfully the Swedish version. It was the called *The Cellist*, featuring the delightful Pontus and Isabelle. The one in which Kurt most beautifully bares his soul. His dog Jussi features too. I crawled into bed, covered up and lost myself in the story. Great drama. The best! I watched it through and tried to sleep. I was in the deepest, dark turmoil but I did eventually manage to drop off.

I was woken at about 3:00am by a knock on my door. I jumped out of bed and scrambled across the room, tripping over my trousers and shoes. I almost crashed into the door with a muffled "Hi."

"It's me, Susie."

Ah, relief. I swung open the door and we clutched each other, hugging tight like we'd been apart for a century.

"I love you, Susie. I love you, I love you."

"I love you too, John."

The day started bright. White, puffy clouds raced across the sky. I couldn't help but look for familiar shapes in them. Anything: animals, land masses, faces. It was just a thing I did at times to amuse myself.

Susie was watching me with my eyes on the sky. "Clouds are not spheres," she said and smiled.

I didn't get what she meant, but I felt my mood lift a notch when I caught that smile and managed to creak one back.

"You, what?" Biro responded a bit too confrontationally for my liking. I wanted to keep things sweet and get back on track.

"Clouds are not spheres, mountains are not cones, bark is not smooth and lightning does not travel in straight lines." Susie leaned back in her seat.

Biro looked unimpressed. "At the risk of stating the glaringly obvious. Bark is not smooth, Jesus!"

"Sure, Biro, it's obvious, I agree, but in my line of work that's a worthwhile observation."

"Why?"

"I've been telling John all about this. It's important because we've now got a geometry, which can describe these things."

"Which is?"

"Fractal geometry, Biro."

"Never heard of it, Susie."

"Hardly surprising. It was only developed towards the end of the last century."

"What is it?" March spoke for the first time that day.

"Well, March, it's like this: it took a long time for us to emerge and start to look out at the physical, observable universe not as a narrow, separate little entities, but rather being able suddenly to look out at the totality of nature, and then say, I'll be damned, we've got nothing—no geometry—to describe it with. Clouds are not made with straight edges. Right? And, I'm sure you'll agree, that trees are not circles, they're not triangles. They're something very different indeed. There's a continual kind of a pattern that I can see as I look at the edge of a rising cumulus cloud like that one." She pointed out her side window and we all turned to look. "It's very wrinkly and coruscated and has such fine structure in it, doesn't it? And you would have to agree that there're no lines or circles there. The wonderful discovery that allows us to measure these irregular natural phenomena is an extension of classical Euclidean Geometry. It's called Fractal Geometry."

"Ah ha", March responded. I wasn't sure if he got it or not. Biro simply looked puzzled. I thought I understood what she was getting at. It wasn't rocket science.

We parked in the tree-lined hollow. I switched off the engine and we sat in silence. Biro laid the ordnance survey map on his lap while he googled a satellite view.

March looked around vaguely. "As Quentin Tarantino would say, where the fuckin' fuck are we?"

I chortled, "In the boonies, March."

"You don't say, John."

Biro ignored him. "The location we head for is here." He pointed out a spot on the map as he leaned over the front seat. He traced a line from the car up toward the house. "Here to here. We'll set off from this point, fan out and observe. March and I will skirt round the whole building, noting all ways in and out then find a spot to watch the front of the house from. Point is, we have to do whatever we can to establish who's in there and how many of them there are. So it may be a long wait. Maybe the whole day. If we don't feel sure at close of play that we know everything we could know we come back tomorrow. Any thoughts?" He looked round the car. No comments. "OK. Now did everyone charge their phones?"

Susie and I nodded but March looked guilty. "I forgot."

"Any charge at all on it?" Biro asked with a sigh.

"Doubt it." March sulked.

"Boy, oh boy, March. You certainly take the biscuit. For fuck's sake do it tonight. They're our only way to communicate at a distance. You may not have noticed yet, but we don't have radios," Biro added with heavy sarcasm.

March scowled but said nothing. No apology. There was tension between the two men and, along with many other things that bothered me. I wanted it to be all for one and one for all, but maybe that was just my musketeery wishful thinking. Groups of human beings never seemed to stay harmonized for long. I knew that from my own short, slightly bitter experience. I didn't fancy tackling March or Biro about it head on. I don't like confrontation. Never have.

Remembering his earlier comment and trying to lighten things up I turned to look round at March. "Didn't take you for a movie fan, March."

"Ah well, I never cease to surprise! Yeah, I like the movies. Go almost every week."

"You like Tarantino's flicks?" asked Susie.

"Nah, not much. He's like Orson Welles, Susie."

She turned to look at him. "What d'you mean?"

"They both lived their lives backwards."

"Backwards?"

"Yup, Susie, backwards."

"Explain please, March."

"Well, Susie, it's like this. Orson Welles started out directing one of the greatest films ever, namely *Citizen Kane*, and ended his career doing voice-overs for sherry commercials. Tarantino started out with *Reservoir Dogs* and winds up giving us *Inglourious Basterds*."

"Well, March," I put in, "maybe he's not finished yet."

"We can but live in hope, John. We can but hope."

We all laughed. It cheered me up. I climbed out of the car and walked round to the boot. I started to unload the groundsheets, binoculars, vacuum flasks etc. and thought again about the guns. They were, I knew, in Biro's backpack. He joined me, poured water in the kettle, broke out the stove and lit it. He walked off to one side, broke out his phone and dialed. I heard my phone ring. I answered and heard Biro's voice, "Just checking that we get a signal up here." He turned to me and nodded. He dialed again and Susie's phone rang. Then mine's. "Good." He switched off and pocketed his phone.

We waited in silence for the water to boil while Biro spooned coffee in to the flasks and set them out on the ground. I looked out over the landscape. I knew where the house was, but couldn't see it.

Once the water had boiled Biro filled up the flasks, put on their lids and handed them out. He crammed a groundsheet, raincoat and vacuum flask in his bag and zipped it with a nod to me. I knew what he meant. We followed suit and loaded our packs. I put on my big US Army issue coat with all the pockets. It was a favourite of mine and it gave me some comfort. I needed that. There was tension in the air. The mood wasn't all that good.

Susie took the initiative, "Cheer up, boys, it ain't happened yet." She looked pointedly at March. He managed a weak smile and turned away.

As we moved off I noticed that the clouds were slowing, bulking up and turning dark. I didn't recognize anything familiar up there now. We moved forward in line with Biro walking point with me taking up the rear. Biro's head swung from left to right and back again constantly. Sometimes he looked down but rarely at his feet. They found sound footing instinctively. It started to rain. Steadily. The cloud base lowered rapidly and visibility was quickly reduced to 100 yards. Biro stopped and I walked up the line to confer with him. Susie and March unpacked their raincoats and put them on.

"This will work in our favour, John. It increases our cover an hundredfold."

"An hundredfold?"

"Just a turn of phrase. D'you like it?"

"Indeed I do, Biro."

"We will need to find hides closer to the house under these circumstances which is, of course, a big plus."

I got his drift and I felt the confidence start to flow back into my boots as I went back to the end of the line and we continued our way through the rain. It was strangely beautiful landscape with its many and varied tones of green and grey. Biro turned to us, signaled for silence and for us to stop while he listened intently. I could hear nothing but the swish of rain and the rushing of water in the brook, which ran alongside our path. He waved for us to move again and we sloshed on through the rain, squelch after squelching step.

After another hundred yards Biro held up his hand again and the column came to a halt. He signaled for us to gather round him. Keeping his voice down he instructed Susie and me to head for the right side of the house and then find a suitably secure spot to observe from. He told us to keep low and to put our phones on the vibrate setting. He repeated that he and March would first circle the house and then take up a position on the left of the building. He asked us to call him when we were in position. Except for March we all took out our phones and set them to vibrate. With an encouraging nod he and March headed off into the rain. I heard the distinct, heavy click of Biro sliding back the breech, arming one of the handguns. I felt better off without one. Susie and I went off in search of a hide, keeping low as we went.

We skirted round a clump of small, windblown trees and the house came into view. It was a large, imposing grey building—austere and cold. All was quiet. There was no activity outside. Smoke curled and spiraled lazily out of one tall chimney, making difficult progress upward in the heavy rain. Susie and I found a small hollow bordered by a rocky outcrop and took out our groundsheets, spreading them with difficulty on the uneven ground. I phoned Biro and confirmed that we were in position. We settled down to watch. We soon appreciated that, as Biro had planned, we were at the back of the house. Using the binoculars we could see rubbish bins of various colours, a coal bunker, a log pile and some axes. I didn't like the look of them! I didn't fancy being axed. I shuddered at the thought of it. I decided that if it came to it a bullet would definitely be preferable to being hacked and cut up.

Huddled in that dip in the ground with Susie I was suddenly deliriously happy. This was as good as it gets. Maybe this would be as good as it would get. The future seemed very uncertain just then.

I took my flask out of my bag and poured a cup of black coffee, offering Susie the first go. We took turns watching the house with our binoculars. Although we were there for several hours the time went fast.

Susie kept me entertained with her mathematics. "Think about it, John, like I said nature makes things that are not smooth-edged and regularly shaped like cones, circles, spheres and straight lines etc." She paused. "Look around you. The real world is wrinkled, crinkled, and irregularly shaped. It's a wiggly world! It's amazingly though that, until so recently we didn't have a geometry to describe our natural world. But, as I explained, we do now all thanks to Benoît Mandelbrot. Just like you, John, he was a visionary and a maverick. He made connections that others failed to do. He took a very bold and difficult step. I admire him greatly. In fact I am probably one of his most devoted fans."

She allowed me the time to ponder on what she had said as I looked at the world around us. It was indeed mostly wiggly as far as I could see. Around midday after I had taken a pee we broke out bread and cheese from our bags and had a satisfying, simple, if wet, lunch. At all times Susie kept an eye on the house.

After we had eaten I went back to observing. An hour passed and there was still no movement around the house. The smoke, though, continued to curl up from the chimney so someone was certainly feeding the fire. I sat back and let Susie take a turn. Keeping her eyes on the house she asked me, "And what about pi, John?"

"And what about pi, Susie?"

"As you probably know, John, pi represents a number, which describes the relationship of the circumference of a circle to its diameter. But amazingly what that number is exactly remains undiscovered. In ancient times mathematicians worked it out to hundreds of decimal places and now with computers we've done it to many millions of places, but without finding a regular pattern or any whole-number fraction between a circle's circumference and its diameter. So there is in fact no such thing."

"No such thing?"

"That's right. Pi is a string of numbers starting 3.141592654 and going on forever. In fact, you see, there's no such thing on earth as a perfect circle. Pi is truly a transcendental number without resolution. So in that respect it's like the Mandelbrot set, don't you think?"

"Yes, I guess it is." I wanted her to go on, but she had made her point and lapsed into an easy silence. She slipped away into the bushes to pee I presumed.

We took turns observing throughout the afternoon. The rain stopped and the sun peeped out now and again through the broken, racing clouds. I felt my phone vibrate in my pocket. It was Biro. He suggested we pull back to the car and call it a day. We skulked back to the track in the deepening twilight.

As we walked, Susie whispered, "I think you'll like this John. The famous and remarkable theoretical physicist Paul Dirac once said, One could perhaps describe the situation by saying that God is a mathematician of a very high order, and he used very advanced mathematics in constructing the universe."

"Yes, Susie. That is poetry. So it must be true." I thought that if she was comfortable with that idea she would probably accept me having a guru.

When we reached the car March and Biro were already there. We shuffled to the back and I unlocked the boot. We loaded our bags and got into the car.

"Let's have the heating on please, John." March was shivering and showing his age I thought. I switched on the engine and cranked up the heater. The car started to warm up quickly and I put her into reverse to turn round, then started to drive back to the hotel.

Biro was pensive and I could tell he wanted to say something. "What's up, Biro?"

"There was a '35 Convertible Hispano-Suiza parked out front. Beautiful. Cream and brown."

"And what's a Hispano-Suiza?" I asked.

"It's a Spanish deluxe limousine. Probably the most deluxe limo ever made. And I know *that* car. I know who owns it."

"How come?"

"There are so few left in the world."

I was intrigued "But how the hell d'you know whose it is, Biro?"

"The guy who owned it then—and he said he would never sell it—was pay-rolling the Hungarian band I roadied for on the US tour. I mean, it may not be the same guy, but my gut feeling is that it is. He was so attached to it. He totally loved it."

"And his name was?"

"He called himself Velus Chrome. I didn't think for a minute it was his real name."

"It wasn't," I responded.

"What is it, then, John?"

"I was told that it was Tigran Gevorkian."

"Sounds more likely."

I was intrigued. "Did he tell you how he made the money to buy that car?"

"Oh, yes. He was very boastful, very full of himself. Said he was a metal trader . . . unsurprisingly, I guess, going by a name like Chrome. I didn't trust him. It was unbelievably difficult to get our wages out of him. In fact we never did."

"Never?"

"Never, John. What a slimebag! That man owes me big time, I can tell you."

I looked over my shoulder at Biro, "As William Burroughs once said: 'Money is always slow in coming'."

"Now, there's a writer I do know."

"Thought you would, March."

Chapter Twenty Six

IT'S JUST A RIDE

**"And what you ask was the beginning of it all.
And it is this: existence that multiplied itself for
sheer delight of being so that it
might find itself innumerably."**
Sri Aurobindo

No one had come out of the house at all during the day so we had no more to go on regarding numbers. In that sense it had been a fruitless day, but I had enjoyed my time with Susie in that endless, gloomy rain.

To lighten things up a bit on the way back to the hotel I asked everyone for their favourite band or solo artist.

March was the first to respond. "The Johnny Hitchcock All Star Big Band."

"I beg your pardon?" I turned round to look at March.

"The Johnny Hitchcock Band. No one heard of them?"

We all shook our heads.

"They were big in the late '50s."

Biro laughed. "And where was that March?"

"New Mexico, Biro."

"Ah well, March, that explains it."

"Explains what?"

"Why none of us have heard of 'em," I put in.

March looked wistful. "They were in the Glenn Miller tradition. Swing. You know, the big band sound."

"Yes. OK. I'd say we've all heard of Glenn Miller, March," Biro responded in an off-hand kind of way.

March shrugged. "Yeah, well, I guess . . ."

"What about you, Susie?"

"Uh . . . difficult, John. Let me think about it."

"OK . . . Biro?"

"Czech band."

"Called?"

"Anal Rape."

Susie spluttered, "You're kidding, Biro."

"Yeah. I'm kidding, Susie."

"Glad to hear it."

"I really prefer The Foreskin Five."

"Jesus!" It was March this time.

I tried to keep things going. "So what really is your favourite band, Biro."

"Iron Maiden."

"What! You're pulling our legs again, Biro," Susie retorted.

"No, I'm not. I mean it, Susie."

"But they're . . ."

"Heavy metal. Good combat music. Gets you psyched up. I got hooked on them in The Regiment and have never managed to kick the habit."

Susie shook her head in disbelief. "What about you, John?"

"Oh, I'm pretty predictable, Susie."

"Go on then."

"Robert Zimmerman."

"Robert who?" Biro was genuinely puzzled.

"Robert Zimmerman."

"Who's he?"

"Come on, Biro."

"I really don't know."

"Famous Jewish singer-songwriter."

"Yeah, well, I got the Jewish bit, but who is this Zimmerman, John?"

"Bob . . ."

"Bob who, John?"

"Oh, come on, Biro. Bob 'who'?"

"Dunno."

"The troubadour/poet. The voice of the 60s . . ."

"Nope."

I laughed. I was enjoying this, but finally gave in. "Bob Dylan."

Susie laughed. "Yes, John, you are predictable. I think I could've guessed that."

"How come?"

"You're a writer and you like words."

"He has written some good tunes too, you know, Susie."

"Yes, I know that, but he's mostly words."

March shrugged. "Never much liked his music."

"How can you say that, March? He *was* the voice of his generation."

"So they say."

"So I say, March."

"We haven't heard from you yet, Susie. I'm just wondering what music a mathematician would go for. Bach perhaps?"

"Yes, I love Bach, John. And the fugues are mathematically perfect, but for a lighter touch I'd go for Coldplay."

"Cold Play? Never heard of them."

"You're kidding now, March."

"No, I'm not, Biro. And I'd be the first to admit I'm just not in touch with modern music."

"You can say that again."

We drove on in silence for a couple of miles.

"I was thinking . . ."

"Don't strain yourself, John."

"Oh March, come on. You're having a good ride with John."

I loved her more and more with every passing minute. "Funny you should say that, Susie. I was remembering Bill Hicks and his stand-up act when he does the piece known as 'It's just a ride'."

"I remember it . . . vaguely. How's it go?" asked Biro.

"Hang on. I'll just get it back in my head." I actually knew the whole piece off by heart but only gave them a brief clip and, putting on my best American accent, I launched in: "The world is like an amusement park and, when you choose to go into it, you think it's real because that's how powerful our minds are. And the ride goes up and down and round and round and it has thrills and chills and it's very brightly coloured and it's very loud. And it's fun for a while. Some people have been on the ride for a long time and they begin to question: 'Is this real? Or is it just a ride?' And other people have remembered, and they come back to us and they say: 'Hey! Don't worry. Don't be afraid—ever—because . . . this is just a ride. And we kill those people!"

"That's just brilliant, John." Biro was impressed. "Thank you."

"It's tragic though—his story." I managed to extricate myself from my American accent with difficulty. There were quite enough Americans in the car already.

March started to take an interest at the mention of the word 'tragic'. "Why?"

"He died when he was only 32 and we lost most probably the best and smartest comedian of his generation. The point I wanted to make from all this is that this mission—or whatever you want to call it—is just a ride for you three. I guess it is for me too, but I have a very distinct purpose driving me. I appreciate you all wanting to help me out with this one and I know you're here voluntarily, but can I say that if any of you want to pull out now I'd understand. We are getting near the final deal and someone might get hurt . . . really . . . and not just one of them, but any of us. So speak now or forever hold your peace." I waited.

"I'm in."

"I thought you would be, Biro. How 'bout you, March?"

"I'm in too."

"And you, Susie?"

"I'm in all the way, John. Most exciting thing I've done in years."

"What about the danger?"

"I'll take it as it comes. I won't lose my bottle, John. Don't worry."

"Good. We'll go for it then. All for one and one for all."

Chapter Twenty Seven

THE AK47 AND THE THREE DS

**"Lieutenant General Mikhail Timofeyevich
Kalashnikov (born November 10, 1919 in Russia's
Southern Altai region) most famous for designing the
AK-47 assault rifle."**
Wikipedia

In my early 20s I read over 40 memoirs written by soldiers and airmen, who'd fought in the Vietnam War. It became an obsession with me. One of my favourites was *Sympathy for the Devil* by Kent Anderson. I particularly liked *The 13th Valley*, by John M del Vecchio and *Chickenhawk* by Robert Mason. The former tells a blow-by-blow account of a platoon on a week-long patrol in the jungle. And the latter is a memoir of a helicopter pilot, who flew slick Hueys in terrifying and demanding conditions—conditions that called for deep wells of courage and unbelievable piloting skills.

I wrote a short story called *Victor Charlie* about a Vietcong freedom fighter, living in the extensive tunnel network from where the VC fought the war. This was a story of self-sacrifice where the hero gives his life to save his friend and one-time enemy.

I picked up a lot of the American soldiers' slang for a host of different things: for their weapons, the heat, the food, the pain, the horror and the rare moments of joy. There was murder and mayhem and a lot of fear. There was poetry too. John Helm, a US Marine Private in the Ashau Valley in South Vietnam in 1969 wrote this combat haiku—all negative space and darkness, humming with portent:

'Patrol went up the mountain. One man came back. He died before he could tell us what happened.'

Young grunts referred to men with just a few days of their tour left to survive as 'single digit midgets'. A cock-up was a 'clusterfuck', or a 'boondoggle'. A badly injured grunt was described in brief as being 'fubar'. Fucked up beyond all recognition.

I can recall a truly bizarre sequence in a low-budget British Vietnam War movie called *How Sleep the Brave*. The film was shot on location in Buckinghamshire and cost peanuts. Nonetheless it has some excellent scenes. In one of them an Army platoon under Lieutenant No-hands (so-called because he cuts the hands off prisoners) are burning down a village for no good reason. Two small boys come up to a group of soldiers setting fire to a thatched house. One of the soldiers turns to the boys and taking out a stick of sweets asks, "Hey kid, wanna Tootsie-roll?"

The boys stare amazed at the soldier and of them quips, "Fuck you, cheap Charlie," and walks off.

I also read avidly stories of airmen flying Spitfires, Hurricanes and Lancaster Bombers—particularly Lancasters—in the Second World War. I wrote a story I called *No Greater Love*. It was about a Lancaster crew who were flying on a big bombing raid to Hamburg in a plane that was not their own called M-Mother. They called their own Lanc Creaking Door because those planes creaked and groaned all the time. Especially during take-offs and landings. M-Mother was part of an armada of nearly 150 aircraft taking part in a series of coordinated raids on Hamburg over 48 hours in July 1943 designed to set the city on fire. The attack went by the name of Operation Gomorrah. The RAF bombed at night and the USAF with their Flying Fortresses during the day. Over 30,000 civilians were literally greased—incinerated or asphyxiated—in the ensuing firestorm, which the bombing produced. Cars, bicycles and bodies literally melted in the heat. The planes' bomb-bays were loaded with bombs that were 50% high explosive and 50% incendiaries. It was high summer and the wind was blowing hard. The fire-storm raged for several days and nights. From the point of view of the allies the raid was a success. It was what I would, however, call a pyrrhic victory.

A German ME 110 Nightfighter pilot had lost his family in a bombing raid and he had decided that he would take out a Lancaster that night in revenge. In my story the battle between the ME 110 and M-Mother raged from above the suburbs of Hamburg out across Germany, France and the North Sea. The German pilot almost managed to down the Lancaster many times, reducing her to one engine, killing three of the six-man crew. After the German had used up all his ammunition he even tried to ram the tail of the Lanc almost forcing her into the sea. He followed the crippled bomber until she was right over her own airfield. M-Mother was able to manoeuvre herself to shoot down the damaged 110, which crashed in flames. The pilot of the Lanc risked his own life pulling the German pilot from his burning aircraft. Another tale of self-sacrifice. This is clearly a continuing theme in my writing.

Homer wrote:

> "That courage, which the gods breathe into the souls
>   of heroes,
> Is borne of man's love of his own nature, infused into
>   the lover.
> Love will make men die for their beloved—love alone."

I put away a fair number of books by fast jet pilots flying in Vietnam too. Those guys have a name or a phrase for nearly everything. I read *Phantom Over Vietnam* by Marine Corps pilot Colonel John Trotti. When one of the pilots in his squadron drove his plane nose-first into the ground killing him and his weapons officer, Trotti referred to this as 'whiffflediff'! There's a brilliant passage where he describes the qualities of the F-4 Phantom, which was the aircraft he flew on operations:

'We were two-thirds of the way down the runway—abeam our squadron area—when the airspeed needle passed 310 knots and I pulled into a 2.5-g climbing arc, looking to lay the airplane on its back in a 45 degree climb, heading feet wet over the coastline. It was hotdogging, but the troops loved it—and, even if they didn't, I did! We were inverted, coming up on 400 knots as we rocketed past 2000 feet, still looking straight down the flight line. This had been what the engineers at McDonnell had in mind when they first put pencil to paper. Despite the fact that the word is grossly overused, it's awesome. If you stop for a moment and imagine the wildest, fire-breathingest, farthest-out thing in the world, and then let your imagination out one more notch, you've got it indexed. A healthy Phantom hauling buckets in its element.'

Then there were those famous lines spoken by Lieutenant Colonel Bill Kilgor (played by Robert Duvall) in *Apocalypse Now* following a US Army helicopter cavalry group assault on a Viet Cong outpost at the mouth of the Nung River. When all the grunts were sitting around camp-fires on the beach that evening one of them asks Kilgore why they took the area, to which he replied, 'Charlie don't surf!' The next day Kilgore was striding shirtless along the beach in his cavalry officer's Stetson hat. He took a deep breath and exclaimed, 'I love the smell of napalm in the morning. You know, one time we had a hill bombed, for twelve hours . . . The smell, you know that gasoline smell, the whole hill. Smelled like victory.'

My thoughts on this were: Men love their weapons too, not simply for keeping them alive, but for a deeper reason. They love their rifles and their knives for the same reason that the mediaeval warriors loved their armour and swords: they are instruments of beauty. Art and war were for ages as linked as art and religion. Mediaeval and Renaissance artists gave us cathedrals, but they also gave us armour, sculptures of war, swords and muskets and cannons of great beauty—art was offered to the gods of war as reverently as the carved altars were offered to the gods of love! Like John Lennon sang 'Happiness is a Warm Gun'.

When an RAF pilot crashed and burnt his plane, his crew and himself it was often referred to as a 'prang'. Notably, one of the reasons for the RAF won The Battle of Britain, which was fought in the skies over Southern England in the latter half of 1940, was because the young British pilots flew Spitfires and Hurricanes. Whereas on the other side the equally young Luftwaffe pilots flew the Messerschmitt ME 109. Now the word 'Messer' means 'one who measures' and 'schmitt' means, well, 'schmitt'. Probably translates as 'Smith'. So no chance against the Spitfire and the Hurricane with a name like that!

It's in the meaning of the words, but more in the sound they make. The pop, pop, pop of the Kalashnikov. The crack of the M16. The rattle of the SA80. The name 'Kalashnikov' had as onomatopoeic quality. KALASH!—it somehow sounds like a round being fired from an automatic weapon. BTW: The A in AK stands for 'Automat'. It's weatherproof. Works in dust, mud, sand, arctic and desert conditions. It's ubiquitous. It's absurdly simple to strip and clean. It is known as the 'peasants' weapon'. It's brilliantly engineered and was created by Mikhail Kalshnikov in 1947 while he was in hospital recovering from injuries he caught in the World War II. The fact that it was designed in the middle of the last century and has never needed to be upgraded or altered in any way indicates the simplicity and effectiveness of the weapon. I often wonder how Kalashnikov felt about the weapon he created when he learnt about its spread throughout the world and the amount of suffering it has doled out and continues to dole out to this day.

Biro kept a watch on the drive back to the hotel looking, I presumed, for men in black water-proofs and sou'westers. In any event we didn't see anyone looking even vaguely like that. In fact we hardly saw anyone. Just a couple of cars going in the opposite direction. One was driven by a nodding white-head and the other by a girl, who looked like she was still in her teens. So, nothing to worry about there.

Nonetheless I caught myself fretting again as we drove back through the town and had to attempt to heave myself out of that hole.

March rescued me from the downward spiral, "You know what 3D is, Biro, yes?"

"Yeh. Course I know what 3D is."

"OK, but do you know what the 3Ds are?"

"Nope, March, I don't."

"They are: drugs, dogs and dollars."

"Yeah, OK, March, but you don't have any drugs, do you?"

"No."

"And you don't have a dog do you?"

"No."

"So?"

"So I would have both if I had me some dollars, Biro."

"So dollars should be the first D then."

"Yes, Biro, I guess you are dead to rights on that one though I'd rather have pounds if that word began with a D." They chuckled. Susie smiled at me and I immediately felt a whole lot better. That smile on its own worked wonders, but the fact that March and Biro had something going now really was the icing on the proverbial cake.

"You know there's a D in £SD, of course," I pointed out thoughtfully.

"Ah, let's get high and do the infinite," quipped March. I kept my experiences with that mystical liquid to myself for the time being.

"Yeah, could do, March, if we had the wherewithal." Biro nudged him. Susie didn't look impressed. She gave me a sideways look.

"Mind you, that D is only for pennies so it might not amount to very much." And that was my final comment on the subject as we rolled into the hotel car park.

We sat still for a while, quietly checking the scene. A young couple went by with a Golden Retriever. They looked so happy and it got me thinking about dogs. I have always loved them and, as a child, I was never without a dog. Always had one in fact until I got together with Amelia and my beautiful Cavalier King Charles Spaniel I called Jezebel had to go on account of Amelia's asthma and her allergies. It was heart-breaking, but I had to give up one love to catch another. A beautiful little story I once heard floated back into my mind and, before I knew it, I was telling the others.

"There once lived a king called Dharmaputra, who was the soul of virtue and compassion. When the time came for him to shed his body he went up to heaven with his dog. When he reached heaven's gate the guardian looked up his name. "Let's see . . . Dharmaputra. Yes, we have orders to let you in. But we don't have any listing for a dog."

"Won't you please look again?" Dharmaputra asked.

So the guardian looked again, "I'm sorry, but there is no provision here for dogs."

Dharmaputra did not hesitate for a second. "The dog loves me and I love him", he said. "Wherever I go, he goes too. I have to take him with me!"

So the guardian looked again at all the relevant rules and records. "Rules are rules," he said finally. "Either you come in alone, or you go back."

Dharmaputra did not budge. He said simply, "No dog, no me."

Then a miracle took place. Suddenly instead of a dog it was Sri Krishna, the God of Love, standing at Dharmaputra's side. The amazed guardian opened the gates immediately and, as Dharmaputra entered heaven, Sri Krishna leaned over and whispered, "That was a close shave, wasn't it?"

They listened in silence then they all laughed. I could see it had affected them on two levels. We left the car without speaking, collected our gear from the boot and went on into the hotel.

Chapter Twenty Eight

EIGHTY

"Judas pointed down the road
And said, 'Eternity'
'Eternity?' said Frankie Lee
With a voice as cold as ice.
'That's right', said Judas Priest, Eternity
Though you might call it Paradise.'
"I don't call it anything"
Said Frankie Lee with a smile
'All right', said Judas Priest,
'I'll see you after a while'."
Bob Dylan

80 is my lucky number. Boringly and, perhaps predictably, since 1980 is the year of my birth. But it's a good number. As Susie explained to me, placed on its side 8 is the symbol for infinity. Zero is a fascinating number too and it has a bit of a history. The ancient Greeks, she told me, were unsure about the status of zero as a number. They asked themselves, 'How can nothing

be something?' leading to philosophical and, by the Mediaeval period, religious arguments about the nature and existence of zero and the vacuum. The paradoxes of Zeno of Elea mostly depend on the uncertain interpretation of zero. The concept of zero as a number and not merely a symbol for separation is attributed to India where, by the 9th century AD, practical calculations were carried out using zero, which was treated like any other number, even in division. The Indian scholar Pingala and others used the Sanskrit word sunya to refer to zero or void.

Next day found us out at the coast again. This time Biro broke out the guns. He handed me the Sig. Susie and I made our way around the back of the house and while it was still out of sight we climbed to the top of a rise. The sky was abruptly torn apart as two silver Tornado F3s roared low over our heads from out of nowhere almost popping my ear-drums. Susie opened her arms in welcome. The planes were gone in seconds. There's something about those fast jets and the way they sound and shake your bones that literally makes your hair stand on end. We laughed out loud in the echoing boom. Still grinning we scrambled into our hide and made ourselves as comfortable as we could.

While we waited and with Susie watching the house I pulled my worn and battered copy of the Rig Veda out of my bag and opened it up at my favourite page. I was seldom without this book. "Can I read you this?" I asked,

"Sure. What is it?"

I held out the book for her to see. She took her eyes off the house for a few seconds to glance at it and nodded. "I've heard of it, but never read it."

"Listen to this then, Susie. See what you think." I moved closer to her, into the sphere of new-mown hay and whispered, "There was not then what is nor what is not. There was no sky, and no heaven beyond the sky. What power was there? Where? Who was that power? Was there an abyss of fathomless waters? There was neither death nor immortality then. No signs were there of night or day. The one was breathing by its own power in deep peace. Only the one was; there was nothing beyond. Darkness was hidden in darkness. The all was fluid and formless. There in the void, by the fire of fervour arose the one. And in the one arose love. Love, the first seed of soul. The truth of this the sages found in their hearts: seeking in their hearts with wisdom, the sages found that bond of union between being and non-being. But who knows in truth? Who can tell us whence and how arose this universe? The gods are later than its beginning; who knows therefore whence comes this creation? Only that god who sees in the highest heaven. He only knows whence comes this universe, and whether it was made or uncreated. He only knows, or perhaps he knows not."

Susie looked round at me briefly and whispered, "Hey cowboy, that's pretty good. It's beautiful. Poetic."

"I think so."

"I'll you something else about poetry, John, my boy, which I bet you've never ever thought of."

"What's that?"

Keeping her eyes on the house she said, "The best mathematicians are poets. In the middle of the 19th century a mathematician called Karl Weierstrass said: 'A mathematician who is not also something of a poet will never be a perfect mathematician.' How 'bout that?"

"Well, that that's good to hear, Susie. It broadens things out."

"So your turn again. Tell me more about the Rig Veda." She went back to watching the house.

"It's one of the oldest sacred texts in the world. It's reckoned that it dates from somewhere around1500 BC. Apart from the piece I just read you it contains several other accounts of the origin of the universe."

"How come you know about it?"

"I've been to India a couple of times and I have a . . . uh . . . spiritual guide . . . a guru." I was hesitant because I thought she might not take to this.

"You do?"

"Yup, Susie, I do."

"Tell me about him—it is a him is it?"

"It is a him. But I'll leave going into that for another time, if you don't mind." Thinking about my guru at this time and in this place made me feel uneasy and vaguely guilty. I had to put him out of mind. Not an easy thing to do.

"I'm OK with that, John. Whenever you feel like it is fine by me."

I snapped the book shut. I had seen a movement out of the corner of my eye. Susie was already alert, staring hard at the house through her binoculars. "What can you see?" I whispered.

"There are two men in the yard. They're collecting logs."

"One tall, big and hairy and one skinny little one?"

"For sure."

"Nothing and Everywhere!" I knew we had arrived. This was the right place. Somewhere in that house was my computer, my novel. I knew it. I felt anger and outrage pour through me. I wanted to go right down there and blast them to bits, but I held myself in check.

We watched the two men go back and forth with logs a few times. After they had finished carting, they both stood outside for a while smoking. I just wished I could hear what they were saying. I called Biro and told him what we had seen. He sounded weighed down. Bothered.

"What is it, Biro?"

"We've got a serious problem. Half an hour ago a big black, wide-wheeled Range Rover swung into the front drive. And two serious heavies got out. Huge, cropped-headed goons. Black suits."

"Shades of Reservoir Dogs," I cut in. Biro grunted, but didn't laugh. "One of them was openly sporting an Uzi." He sounded worried.

"Out-numbered and out-gunned then, Biro."

"You could say."

"What'll we do?"

"Right now we go back to the hotel. Get some rest and come back out here 'round 5am. Before dawn. Maybe they're not staying. I want us to go in as soon as and if that car clears."

We didn't talk for the first couple of miles on the way back. Susie was driving. Eventually Biro spoke. "The Hispano-Suiza was still where it was when we arrived. It hasn't moved."

I pondered our situation for a couple of minutes. "D'you think they both had Uzis?" I asked.

"Dunno. Couldn't tell." Biro shrugged.

"What about you March? Did you see . . . ?"

"I wasn't there. I was peeing when they drove off."

That pretty much closed up the subject until March asked: "Is that Uzi the Israeli sub-machine gun?"

"More of a machine pistol in truth, March." Biro stared out of the window for several minutes. "It's a cool weapon if you like that kind of thing. Small, lightweight. Fires 9mm rounds at up to 600 a minute. Designed by a guy called Uziel Gal round about 1950. The Uzi is an open bolt, blowback. It was one of the first sub-machine weapons to use a telescoping bolt design. The mag is in the pistol grip so it's a short weapon."

"You know a lot about 'em, Biro. You didn't use them in The Regiment did you?"

"Nah. We would've liked. Funny thing . . . the Uzi's been taken up by more militaries than any other submachine gun." He turned back from the window and glanced across at me in a conspiratorial way. I liked his face. It had enormous strength in it. There was a boldness about him, a knowingness. I could tell he'd been there and seen the deepest dark and the best of men.

He looked back out at the passing landscape. "Used to fire them off when we picked 'em up sometimes after contact in Iraq. Quite common there . . . had to hand them in eventually though." He looked wistful.

Chapter Twenty Nine

THE FIRE IN THE EQUATIONS

**"What is it that breathes fire into the equations
and makes a universe for them to describe?"
Stephen Hawking**

Biro took me aside as we crossed the hotel reception. "Word, John?"

"Sure, Biro. See you in a minute, Susie." She waved and started up the stairs.

He led me out into the forecourt and then through a side gate into the garden. The sun was setting. The trees and the grass glowed golden. We stood for a moment to take it in then Biro led me to a bench under the overhanging branches of an ancient yew.

"So what is it, Biro?"

"I have something I think you should see. I was looking at the guns again to see if there were any clues as to where they came from. I took all the rounds out of the Beretta mag and found this folded up tightly inside." Biro put his hand into an inside pocket of his jacket brought out a small paper slip and handed it to me.

I took it and unfolded it. It was a mathematical formula, clearly written with a fine-tipped pen. I looked at it.

E = – VØ – dA/dt

"What the hell is this, Biro?"

Biro studied the symbols for a few seconds and shrugged.

Of course it meant nothing to me either but I felt a wave of excitement. I felt we might be on to something. "I'll show it to Susie. Should mean something to her."

Biro nodded and we went back into the hotel.

Chapter Thirty

FER-DE-LANCE

**"Scalar Energy is generated when electromagnetism
is unified with gravity."
Nikola Tesla**

I went up to Susie's room and let myself in. I sat on the bed and pulled out the note. "Look at this, Susie. Biro found it with the Beretta."

She sat beside me and looked at it for a few seconds then turned to me. "Fer-de-lance."

"What?"

"Fer-de-lance".

"It's got a nice ring to it. Sounds mysterious . . ."

"Yes. It translates as spearhead."

"And that means?"

"It means scalar weapons, John."

"I've never heard 'em."

"Hardly surprising. Governments guard their secret work with full force."

"So, scalar weapons?"

"This really is . . . something . . ."

"What?"

Susie launched off. "Nikola Tesla was a Serb. He was born in 1856. He was an essential driving force in the birth of commercial electricity. His best work was in electromagnetism in the late 19th and early 20th centuries. Tesla's work was the basis of our modern alternating current system. He played a big part in the Second Industrial Revolution, but he is more or less forgotten. Have you heard of him, John?"

"I don't think I have." Something though was tickling away inside my head. Tesla? "Ah, I remember. A film with David Bowie playing him. A lab with huge coils crawling with blue lightning. A ball of blue light sending blue forks across the lab to a second sparkling sphere. Great sequence. Bowie was good too, but I can't remember the name of the film."

Susie went on, "Tesla was the true winner of the War of Currents, but the power and influence of the money behind Westinghouse and the famous Thomas Edison sidelined him and pushed him right off the map. In his time, Tesla was as famous as the most famous inventors, but because he was so eccentric and made seemingly unbelievable and sometimes bizarre claims, he was ostracized and considered mad. He was 86 when he died—completely forgotten and with no money—in a hotel in New York City."

I tried to take it all in while Susie continued, "His unit creates a magnetic flux. It's described in this formula." She waved the paper in front of me. It gives us a description of scalar power and suggests ways to use it."

"Which are?"

"Well, John. One thing is it can make truly awesome scalar weapons. Using a magnetic induction process which creates gravitational field energy they can generate shock waves that can flatten entire cities, overwhelm power supplies, shut down telecommunications and focus down to wipe out just one hard drive . . . and on and on . . ."

"Who has it?"

"The Russians, the Americans, the Chinese, maybe the British. Thing is it's another but much quieter arms race. I'm sure none of the powers want or expect to use these weapons.

They're too powerful and, in any case, wars aren't fought like that anymore. They're deterrents and the deterer with the most sophisticated weapon system is winning the race. That's it. They all just want to win."

"So how come you know so much about this, Susie?"

"I told you there were some very liberal and open-minded people at Berea College. My math professor was Illinois Sartre. He knew about Tesla. His father was a general in military intelligence. Illinois was well connected and well-liked and he could find out whatever he wanted."

"Illinois?"

"His father was French and his mother was Native American Shoshone." She glanced at me. I waited. "Using his wits Illinois penetrated the security net. Inside he had access to weapons' workshops and development facilities for testing and refining scalar weaponry. He realised quickly that what he had seen and learned put him in danger."

"But he was teaching you . . . was he in danger then?"

"No. The technology moved on and what he knew became of less interest to the military. By the time he passed his doctorate he had learned to be very careful who he spoke to about scalar weapons—about electromagnetic/gravity weapons."

"So why'd he tell you, Susie?"

"Because he wanted the unfamiliar math explained and he knew I could do it, John."

"And did you?"

"Sure. I got it and helped him to get it too." She paused and looked at me. "John, my guess is that whatever is hiding on your hard drive is very valuable to some people and very useful to some others and that it has something to do with scalar weapons."

Chapter Thirty One

THE KNOWLEDGE OF GOOD AND EVIL

**"Is this a dagger which I see before me the handle
towards my hand? Or art thou but a dagger of the
mind, a false creation; proceeding from the heat
oppressed brain?"**
William Shakespeare

That night I dreamt I caused my love to die. More of a nightmare
in fact. The soundtrack was Dire Straits' *Romeo and Juliet*. Susie
and I were running down a dingy, narrow street. Either side
grim, run-down tenements stretched upwards into the starless
night. The street was strewn with rubbish. Rain poured down
on us relentlessly. It was mushy underfoot. We were looking for
someone, something. It wasn't clear who or what. We searched
to the left and right for our goal. Like in my Indian dream
with my guru and the AK47 huge cracks started to appear in
the road ahead of us. Hand in hand we vaulted several smallish
chasms until we came face to face with something really deep
and wide. We stepped back to take a run at it. Holding hands
we ran towards it and leapt out into space. I landed clumsily on

the far side, but Susie didn't make it. I kept my balance and held onto her hand. She swung like a pendulum in the dark abyss. I clung to her, trying to find something to hold onto with my other hand. There was nothing. The ground was slimy and I couldn't get a grip on anything. Consumed with fear I looked down at Susie. She smiled back up at me. She looked angelic, calm. She wasn't frightened but I was terrified. Her hand was slowly slipping through my fingers and my strength was running out. The chasm cracked wider, shaking the ground. I slid towards the brink. My strength gave out and I lost my grip on Susie's hand. She slipped away from me, disappearing into the deep dark without a sound. My heart and lungs were bursting. I gasped for air and sobbed. My desolation was total. My body shook and tears poured from my eyes. I wanted to follow her but lacked the courage. I looked into the abyss. Nothing but the blackness. No sound. I slunk off hunched, lost and lonely.

There's nothing more I can add. I leave the deep interpretation to you, dear reader.

Chapter Thirty Two

BLOWBACK

"Blowback is an operating system for self-loading firearms that obtains energy from the motion of the cartridge case as it is pushed to the rear by expanding gases created by the ignition of the propellant charge."
Wikipedia

It was still dark when we swung out from the hotel drive. I had the wheel.

March was singing along in the back seat:

> "Think about a reefer 50 foot long,
> Not too weak and not too strong.
> You'll get high, but not for long,
> If, if you're a viper."

I slid my Best of Elvis CD into the player again and cranked up the volume. We all kicked off when Elvis swung in with All

Shook Up. That car was rocking. As the lyrics poured out over us and Elvis sang, "She touched my hand. What a chill I got. Her lips are like a volcano when it's hot . . ." I turned to Susie and smiled. She looked almost shy for an instant then smiled back with her far-away eyes. We cruised along those country lanes with Elvis as our friend. Two songs later I couldn't help but make a connection to the infinite hotel when Elvis sang, "Although it's always crowded you still can find some room . . ." I paused the CD. Biro and March groaned.

"It's Cantor's infinite hotel, Susie."

"Nice one, John. Heard it said that God's a mathematician and now we know that Elvis is one too!"

"Unless Cantor wrote the lyrics for Heartbreak Hotel. It's a sad song and you did say Cantor was bi-polar."

Susie glanced back at March and I saw him nod and turn away to stare out of his window. "Elvis is God," he added in a low voice.

Biro turned to him. "You could say that, March." He leaned over the front seat. "But what for the love of God's Cantor?"

I felt a bit smug. "He was a mathematician, Biro."

He shrugged dismissively and sat back as we approached the coast. Without Elvis to cheer us along we curled back into our private thoughts as I drove on.

We were parking the SUV in the tree-lined hollow again when March spoke up, "Hey, folks, lighten up. Let me tell you this one. I think it will help. I apologise to you, Susie, in advance just in case, but my guess is you'll like it too."

"Go for it, March. I'm sure I'll be able to take it . . . whatever it is you come up with."

"A man on his Harley was riding along a California beach when suddenly the sky clouded above his head and, in a booming voice, God said, 'Because you have tried to be faithful to me in all ways, I will grant you one wish.' The biker pulled over and said, 'Build a bridge to Hawaii so I can ride over anytime I want.' God replied, 'Your request is materialistic; think of the enormous challenges for that kind of undertaking; the supports required reaching to the bottom of the Pacific and think of the concrete and steel it would take! I can, of course, do it, but it is hard for me to justify your desire for worldly things. Take a little more

time and think of something that could possibly help mankind.'
The biker thought about it for a long time. Finally, he said, 'God,
I wish that I and all men, could understand women; I want to
know how she feels inside, what she's thinking when she gives
me the silent treatment, why she cries, what she means when she
says nothing's wrong, why she snaps and complains when I try to
help, and how I can make a woman truly happy.' God replied:
'You want two lanes or four on that bridge?'"

Susie didn't react. Biro and I laughed. I thought this was a
smart move by March. There was a lighter mood in the car. March
was starting to be useful. He had shoved us into a lighter mood I
thought. Notably Susie hadn't been listening. She obviously had
other things on her mind.

We left Susie at the car and the three of us arrived in one
piece behind a rise close to the front of the house. The sun was
just beginning to lighten the sky. We waited for only about half
an hour before the front door opened and Black Suits came
out and walked towards the Range Rover. They were carrying
shopping bags and Uzis. They clambered into the vehicle and
with a screech of tires drove out of the yard and away down the
drive.

Biro winked and I gave him a thumbs-up. We waited five
minutes and then, satisfied that this was it, Biro waived us forward.
He led us to a low-standing window. He took out his knife and
carefully prised it open. It creaked a bit but the glass didn't
crack. It squeaked too as he swung it open and we scrambled
through onto a cold stone floor. We made our way along a wide
corridor and up some stairs onto the ground floor where we
stood listening for a minute or two. There appeared to be no
movement in the house but that meant nothing if they knew we
were coming, which I believed they did. Ahead of us stood a vast
oak door which Biro cautiously pushed open and peered round.
It was still dark. We heard a movement in the house. They were
coming.

Biro, March and I manœuvered through the great hall. We
heard heavy footfalls heading in our direction. I saw four figures
ducking and weaving in the deep shadows. I thought of the Uzi
and what that could mean, but I slid back the breech and put one
up the spout as quietly as I could. It made a resounding click and

Nothing turned in my direction. I flicked the safety and fired the Sig, aiming high to scare him. It went off with a mighty womp/ crack and the damned thing nearly jumped out of my hand. I farted and the bullet drove into the ceiling. Dust and plaster tumbled down. I had forgotten to hold it with both hands as Biro had advised me. He looked over at me and laughed. March was keeping his head down. I was surprised I hadn't pissed myself. A bullet whizzed by my ear and pinged into the wall just above my head. I ducked down behind a desk.

Biro leapt up, screaming, "Get some!" He loosed off two rounds in quick succession. The four shapes scattered. I saw a flash of flying hair. It had to be Comb-over. I was at the same time shocked and yet not surprised. Things were starting to click together. I got the impression that Biro wasn't shooting to kill, just to intimidate. I felt relieved. It looked good. It felt good. It was very good.

Biro waved for us to move closer to the wall. He slid his hands over the oak panels. He was looking for something. A door, a window or perhaps a light switch. March and I crawled in beside him, keeping low. March was breathing heavily. I slowed my own breathing right down and took in deep gulps of air. The Sig was shaking in my hand. I could still smell the cordite. It'd burned a groove in my nose. The bang and the recoil were overwhelming. It felt like the base of my thumb was bruised. I just hoped I didn't have to use the gun again. I was still prepared to, but I surely didn't want to. My book continued to pull me on with a fierce attraction. Even with Susie in my world I still felt I couldn't live without it. It was my child and I didn't know if it was alive or dead or maybe even injured and in danger. The machine might be dying and closing in on the world beyond. Perhaps time was of the essence and there really wasn't a second to lose.

I moved in tighter to Biro. He continued to fumble like a blind man along the wall until he found what he wanted. He ducked down to whisper to us. "My guess is there're four of them. Nothing, Everywhere, Tigran Gevorkian and the other one who, I guess, must be Comb-over."

"It is, yes," I squeaked back.

"We go on the offensive and push them into a corner. I want us to try and isolate one of them. Preferably Nothing or Comb-over.

Whichever it is we'll threaten him with enough force until he tells us where your computer is. March'll then go with him to fetch it while you and me, John, pin the other three down."

"Got it, Biro." I felt my blood drain into my boots. My head sagged onto my chest. I was terrified.

March snorted. His breathing had slowed right down.

Biro turned to him. "He needn't know you don't have a gun, March. So be tough with him and decisive. Last thing: when we have the machine we'll call Susie and tell her to bring the SUV up to the house. Then we'll make a run for it with our hostage, shooting all the way to keep their heads down if we have to."

He looked round at us and we nodded that we'd got it.

"Surprise is the thing when going on the offensive. I'm going to throw on the lights if this switch works. Follow me, if it does, keeping low and shooting."

The hall was instantly bathed in a low-key, sepia light and we moved fast across the open space to the far wall. I loosed off two rounds as did Biro. I was conscious of starting to count my bullets. The four figures moved smartly towards another huge oak door, which they slipped through, legs flying. We moved on after them, stopping at the doorway to peer cautiously into the next room.

Chapter Thirty Three

KICK, BOLLOCK AND SCRAMBLE

**"There are many here among us,
who think that life is but a joke,
But you and I, we've been through
that and this is not our fate.
So let us not talk falsely now the
hour is getting late."
Bob Dylan**

It didn't start well. It was what we Brits call a kick, bollock and scramble and what the American grunts call a clusterfuck. Either way we pushed off. I tripped on Biro's coat and nearly went for a promenade. March lurched into me, spun off and hit his head on the wall. We got back on our feet, shook ourselves down and ploughed on. I saw the moving silhouettes at the same time as Biro. We both opened up as we charged across the open space towards them. Holding the Sig with both hands I let go two rounds and Biro did likewise. Strangely enough I was getting used to it. We reached the far side of the hall as eight legs scooted out through a huge wooden doorway. We moved quickly after them, pausing at the door to peek out cautiously into the next room. I caught a glimpse of a figure moving across the floor to another door. A loud crack, a flash and a bullet ripped into the wooden doorframe just beside my head, shattering the wood and sending sharp shards and dust stinging into my cheek. I felt blood drooling down and into my mouth but I was OK. Biro pushed through the gap and ran at a crouch across the floor. March was with him. I fired one shot at the far door and, with streaming eyes, followed after them. Biro lunged forward into the shadows and disappeared. There was a crash and sounds of a scuffle. Biro called out for me and I raced towards him. He was rolling over and over on the floor, trying to get on top of the man he was holding down. Again I saw a flying flash of hair and knew who he had. I threw myself into the fray, grabbing Comb-over's flaying left arm. I twisted it and he squealed. Biro looked up, quickly scanning the room. There was no one else in sight. He called March over as he took a length of cord from his coat pocket. He told March to grab Comb-over's right arm and force it behind his back to link up with the left, which I was pulling round. March and I bound his hands while Biro gagged him with a cloth he also took from his coat pocket. We dragged Comb-over back into the hall. Biro clonked him once with the barrel of the Beretta. Comb-over gasped. His bulging eyes watered and his jaw dropped. It must have hurt.

Biro leaned into him. "Listen, you. I am going to take off this gag and you are going to tell me exactly where you are hiding Mr Smith's computer. If you raise your voice or say anything else I shall hit you again. You got it?"

Comb-over nodded vigorously and Biro took off the gag. Comb-over gasped again.

"Now, let's get to it."

Comb-over looked up at Biro. There was a pleading, lost look in his eyes. "You have no idea what he'll do to me if I tell you."

"Shut up."

"Yes, but . . ."

"Shut it."

"Yes, but . . ."

Biro looked across at me and I nodded. I peered round the doorframe into the darkened room. I caught sight of movement, raised the Sig and fired twice. There was a scuffling noise but no return fire.

Biro turned back to Comb-over. "You will come with us."

The poor man looked so relieved I almost felt sorry for him. But Biro was back on his case. "So where is it?"

Comb-over stared blankly back at him.

"Where?"

"I'm thinking."

"Thinking?"

"Trying to remember."

"So?"

"In the machine room . . . up there."

"Are you sure?"

"It's where they put it."

"Can you get there from that direction?" Biro nodded back over his shoulder.

Comb-over nodded. "If you go that way you'll avoid trouble."

"OK." Biro nodded at March. You'll go with him and bring it right back. Biro looked round at Comb-over. "He is armed and if push comes to shove . . . got that?"

"Got it."

"OK. John and I will stay here and hold the fort. Ready?"

"Armed and ready," March responded in true military fashion.

"OK. Hold him by the arm and don't him let go." Biro pulled a bag from his backpack. "The machine goes in here then put it on his back. Make him carry it to us here as quickly as you can." Biro looked around the room and turned to us. "Go!" He pushed Comb-over forward. March grabbed the cop's arm and they moved off, keeping low, letting Comb-over lead the way.

Biro looked at me. I pointed to the part of the room where I had seen the movement and Biro pushed the Beretta into the doorway, firing twice. The gun was near my ear. The flash blinded me temporarily and left my ear ringing like the old bells of Bow. I fired once as Biro single-handedly pushed a heavy chest into the doorway and we took cover behind it. I was impressed by his physical prowess not to mention his courage under fire. I was brim-top-full of fear. He signalled me to come round behind the chest. He stood and opened fire. I saw an abrupt movement in the shadows accompanied by a harsh scream and a harsh voice

I'd not heard before yelling something like: "Sat snorkelem! Naah! Naah! This was followed by a low moan, then: "Armonk!" There was scuffling in the dark. "Armonk!"

I eventually chased these words up online through an Armenian translation service and concluded that he was screaming: "Šat šnorhakal em" and "armownk". The former I later transliterated as: "Thank you very much", and the latter as "Elbow". Elbow turned out to be the case. Biro had shot Tigran Gevorkian in the right elbow rendering him useless as a leader and a fighting force. So now was the time to move in and take more prisoners.

Biro held up his hand. I heard a scuffling behind us. March and Comb-over stumbled into view. I waved them over. Comb-over had the bag on his back. There was a box in it. I pulled them in close to me and pushed my hand into the bag. It felt like a computer. I kissed the bag. Biro handed me his phone and whispered, "Tell Susie to get the car up here *now*."

I was through to her immediately and whispered the message. She confirmed that she got it and I heard the car start up over the phone link.

"You wait here with him, March." He turned to me. "OK, John?" I nodded and started to get on my feet. Biro fired twice into the dark. I saw two figures stand and a high-pitched voice broke the silence. "Don't shoot. We surrender." I had to laugh at the sound of that incongruous screech.

Biro smiled at me as he switched on the room lighting and called out, "Get up slowly and slide your guns across the floor over here."

We heard the guns hit the floor and then a sliding sound. We stood and walked slowly across the room, guns held steadily in our hands. Gevorkian was nursing his blood-soaked arm, his face a picture of pain. Everywhere looked decidedly shamefaced and Nothing was shaking like a leaf. He appeared to have pissed himself. His trousers were distinctly wet around his crotch and down his legs.

"Hello, shit birds. Nice to see you. You gave us a run for our—John's—money, but we got you in the end."

Nothing was white as a sheet. I thought he was going to puke. Everywhere couldn't look me in the eye.

Biro walked over to Gevorkian. "So, Tigran, we meet again and in such *unusual* circumstances." He smiled. Gevorkian snarled.

"Where're the keys to the Hispano?"

"Why?" His accent was thick.

"I want them."

"Why?"

"None of your fucking business, shit-face."

"It's my car."

"Not any more, it isn't, Gevorkian."

"It's worth millions."

"I know and that's why I'm going to have it."

"This is outrageous."

"And so were you, sport: ripping off me, the crew and the band and then to cap it all putting my friend John here through all his pain and strain. Give."

"I can't."

"And why not?"

"The keys are in my trouser pocket."

"Well, get them then, man."

"I can't."

"Get them."

"I can't. They're in my trouser pocket and you've busted my arm."

Biro nodded to March, who walked over to the Armenian and slipped his hand into the trouser pocket. "Yes, they're here. I got them. Ah, and small balls too!"

Gevorkian flinched and yelped. Nothing cringed in sympathy.

Biro took the keys from March. "You've owed me for years, Gevorkian, and it's pay-back time."

"If you take that car and if I ever see you again, I'll kill you."

"Not if I see you first." With one hand holding the Beretta, Biro pulled out four pairs of lightweight handcuffs. He held them out. "'Cuff 'em, please, March

"With pleasure," came the snappy reply.

I was impressed, but very aware that we had to move fast and get out and clear before Black Suits got back.

Chapter Thirty Four

SEMPER FIDELIS

Motto of the US Marine Corps

As we left the house and went into the courtyard Susie drove up and climbed out. "You got it!"

"Yes. I got it and these three rat bags too."

Susie came up to me. She looked concerned. "Are you all right, John?"

"I'm fine. Like they say in the movies, it's only a graze."

She took a paper tissue from the jacket pocket and carefully wiped around my eye and down my cheek. She looked at me intently and kissed me. She held me close. I started to calm down.

"What you gonna do with them, John?"

"Take 'em out into the hills to a really remote spot and dump 'em." I opened my backpack and took out a shirt, which I tore into strips. "Can you help me here, please, Susie?" I walked over to Gevorkian with her and stood behind him. His arm was bleeding but surprisingly not too badly. I pulled a strip of shirt round his back and over his arm. Gevorkian flinched and hissed.

I could almost hear his teeth grinding. Susie threaded it round his elbow a couple of times, then took another strip of shirt and did the same with that. Dextrously she tore the strip down the middle and tied it round the Armenian's arm. I pushed him hard towards Biro, who was over at the Hispano-Suiza, touching it lovingly. "You three in the back now." He waved the Beretta at them again. "Now!"

They climbed into the back seat. It was a big car but it was still a squeeze. Nothing was pushed right into the corner of the seat with Everywhere virtually sitting on top of him.

"Think you can drive this monster, March?"

"Sure, Biro. Love to."

"I'll go with Susie and Comb-over. Follow us." I put my computer most lovingly on the back seat of the SUV and started to clamber into the front. I pushed the Sig into my deep coat pocket.

Comb-over climbed into the back and strapped in. I could see March start the Hispano. Biro sat in the front and watched the trio with his gun trained back on them. Susie got in to drive the SUV. We pulled out of the yard in convoy and headed off. I was nervous, but we got clean away before the Range Rover and Black Suits made it back.

We took a very narrow road deep into the hills and drove for over an hour, leaving the last of the farms far behind. The terrain was wild and the wind howled around us. I turned to look at Comb-over.

"So, Grimsthorne, what's the story?"

Huh?"

"First question is what the hell are you doing here?"

Comb-over stared out the window of the car at the passing hills.

"Yes?"

He looked round at me. "I'm . . . er . . . trying to think where to start . . . how to explain to you . . ."

"Give it a go then."

He took a deep breath and turned to me, "I'm working undercover, Mr Smith."

"No kidding?" Susie turned to me with a questioning look.

"It's true."

"So what are you trying to uncover, Grimsthorne?"

"What that gang is up to." He nodded back to the Hispano.

"Have you found out?"

"I think I have."

"And what are they up to?"

"Well he—Tigran Gevorkian—the other two are just gophers—is buying and selling high-tech military technology."

"Biro worked for him once and he told him his business is making microchips for US Air Force weapons systems."

"Not exactly true. They don't make microchips. What they do is hack in and steal computer programmes, then sell 'em on to the highest bidder."

Susie looked round at Comb-over. "Code?"

He glanced at her. "Yup. Just so."

"Well, that's all gobbledeegook to me," I responded. "Next question, Grimsthorne, is why did he send those two goons to take my computer?"

"Interesting."

"Not interesting. Very irritating."

"I know it must have been."

"OK. So, why?"

"Here it is, Mr Smith. They had some computer code they needed to hide so they picked a common name—sorry—from the London phone book at random and chose you. Then they hacked into your email, which gave 'em the link to your computer. They buried the code so deep in your machine that you wouldn't even know it was there and so nobody else would be able to find it either."

"All right. But why steal the machine?"

"That's very easy to explain."

"Is it? Wow!"

"Yes." He paused for effect.

"Go on, then." I was getting impatient.

"When they wanted to retrieve the code they couldn't get into your computer because your internet connection was down."

"Ironic. It's because I couldn't pay the bill."

"They were going up the wall and were coming under a lot of pressure so they sent in those two goons to steal your machine to get their hands on the code."

"Boy oh boy!" I looked across at Susie and she nodded back.

"And they had fun doing it."

"Now what about the briefcase—all that cash and the Sig-Sauer?"

Comb-over shrugged. "You told me you were going to go through all the skips around your street so I put it there."

"Put it there?"

"That's right."

"Bit risky, wasn't it?"

"Only a bit. It was a risk worth taking."

"So you set me up."

"I did, yes."

"Why?"

"I needed help and I knew you were desperate to get your computer back and that you would do almost anything to achieve that."

"Almost. But I guess you were right on that." I was kind of grateful in a way because without all this happening—without Comb-over's deception—I would not have met Susie—or Biro or March come to that. I turned back to him. "So how come I connected with you at the cop shop? That seems kind of strange to me."

Comb-over looked back out at the passing wildness. "Pure serendipity, Mr Smith. Just chance."

"I find that hard to believe, Grimsthorne."

"It's the truth."

"How do I know you're not a bent copper?"

"You don't."

We drove on in silence. I thought long and hard. Susie said nothing. She left it between me and Comb-over.

Eventually I broke the silence. "What shall I do with the money I have left?"

"You can do whatever you like with it. I can't return it to where it came from."

"Why not?"

"It came from a secret, undeclared slush fund."

"And you don't want any of it, Grimsthorne?"

"No."

"Well, that's a good sign." I watched the landscape unfold layer after layer in the weaving light. "But why so much money?"

"Didn't know what you'd need to do and where you'd need to go to get it back. Follow them to . . . Barbados, Kuwait, Auckland . . . hotels . . . helicopter hire . . ." His voice trailed away.

We drove on for half a mile. Eventually Comb-over spoke again. "What are you going to do with the Sig-Sauer?"

"We're going to dump it and the Berreta and my computer in the sea. We have a boat standing by."

Silence descended again. Susie turned to me. "I believe him, John."

"So do I,"

"We'll have to leave you up here with the other three if you want to continue your deception. You'll have to suffer the same fate I have planned for them."

"Which is?"

"Wait and see."

Chapter Thirty Five

THE EDGE OF CHAOS

**"Self-organisation elaborates in complexity as the
system advances towards the chaotic edge."**
Michael Crichton

I asked Susie to pull off the road and stop the car. The Hispano
came to a halt behind us. I climbed out and walked over to the
limo, opening the back door. Susie and Comb-over followed
me.

"Right, you three. Out."

They stood in a line. Heads bowed. I guess they thought I
was going to kill them. I had the Sig back in my hand. I shoved
Comb-over roughly. He joined the group while Biro uncuffed
them and then untied Comb-over's hands. Gevorkian's arm had
stopped bleeding.

I looked hard at Everywhere. "I'm going to lighten your
load."

He was taken aback.

"Clothes off."

Gevorkian flinched again. "What?"

"You heard me. Clothes off. Now. All of you."

Susie laughed. Biro and March smiled gleefully. Comb-over looked dismayed. It was damned cold up there. Not a tree in sight. No cover. No shelter.

They started to undress. Gevorkian was finding it difficult with his shattered elbow. "You," I pointed at Everywhere, "help him."

Eventually they were all standing there in just their underwear. "I said all your clothes off."

"But," Everywhere yelped, "there's a woman present."

"Big fuckin' deal," smirked Biro gleefully.

"Off!"

Except for Gevorkian they all removed their underwear. I waved the Sig at Everywhere and he got the message. He shuffled self-consciously over to Gevorkian and slid down his boss' boxer shorts. Biro guffawed. March had to turn away he was laughing so much. There they were—all shivering and humiliated in the wicked wind.

I walked up to Everywhere, waving the Sig under his nose in a threatening manner. He went very pale and I could see his knees shaking. I thought he might piss himself. But, unlike Nothing, he didn't. Modesty must have somehow got the better of him.

"So, Everywhere, you or one of your dipsticks somehow hacked into my PC and buried something. Correct?"

"Yes."

"You call me 'Sir' when you speak to me."

"Yes, Sir."

"Better." I walked around him once in an intimidating way. "And that was how you found the name of the novel I'm writing. Am I right?"

"You are, Sir."

Gevorkian snarled at him. I guess there would some difficulties between them later. I hoped so.

I looked hard at Everywhere. "You know you have caused a lot of anguish—a lot of distress."

"Have I?"

"Have I—what?"

"Have I, Sir?"

"Yeah, you and your sidekick here." I glanced across at Nothing, waving the Sig in his direction. It looked like he was going to faint. He did. He pitched forward and fell flat on his face in the heather. I had to laugh as his false teeth flew out of his mouth. I felt like trampling them but I didn't. An image of my guru flashed before my eyes and I was suddenly feeling generous.

Gevorkian turned to Everywhere. He could barely hold himself back from lunging at the big man. "This is your doing. It was your dumb idea to hide the code *there*." His head jerked fiercely in my direction.

"I've explained before, Mr Gevorkian," squeaked Everywhere, "it wasn't me."

"Moron!"

Everywhere squirmed. "Hopescope said he knew what he was doing." He pointed down at Nothing. "And *he* agreed."

Gevorkian groaned. "Oh, my God. There are so many, many ways to hide code easier than that," he muttered.

"Could've created an online site with a unique password," added Susie. "I know that." She walked over to Gevorkian. Biro and I kept our guns on him. She stood in front of him and said: "Spearhead."

Gevorkian didn't respond. He looked steadily at Susie. His eyes were dark and heavy. His face stretched with pain and anger.

"Spearhead." Susie waited then turned to Biro and nodded. Putting on his Regiment face he walked purposefully towards Gevorkian.

"Fer-de-lance?" asked Susie.

"OK. OK . . . yes, Fer-de-lance."

"Fer-de-lance what?"

Biro was nearly on top of him.

"Construction code. Sigma C . . ."

"And?" Susie stared him down.

"Hologram Fractal. Depth 6." He looked like he was going to explode. "We are in deep shit," he groaned.

Biro stepped back

"You can say that again, man." I laughed, looking at them shivering in the gathering gloom.

Gevorkian peered out over the hills at the approaching storm. "There will be a price to pay for this."

"I . . ." Everywhere started to speak, but Gevorkian cut in.

"Shut up. I will sort you out later," he barked. Everywhere looked like he wanted to die. I thought that he probably would soon. Nothing was sobbing quietly on the wet heather. Comb-over's hair was flapping wildly in the wind. I was glad I wasn't him. Or any of them, come to that.

I nodded to the cars. March and Biro went over to the Hispano. I followed Susie to the SUV.

As Biro climbed into the driver's seat he shouted to the group, "Hey, Gevorkian, you know what they say?" He paused for effect. "Payback is a motherfucker!"

Chapter Thirty Six

THE KING AND THE QUEEN OF SWORDS

"Be careful not to touch the wall there's
a brand new coat of paint.
I'm glad to see you're still alive you're
looking like a saint.
Down the hallway footsteps were
coming for the Jack of Hearts."
Bob Dylan

Driving down from the hills I asked Susie what she meant by hiding their stuff securely online.

"Nothing's truly secure, John. Nothing. Look at all the hacking. It goes on all the time. And, if you know how, it's easy."

"So, how's it done?"

"I don't know all the ins and outs of it, but it's known as FTPing your own web space."

"FTPing?"

"It's like this: FTP is short for file transfer protocol. It's a standard *network protocol* used to transfer files from one host to another over the net. FTP is built on a system, which uses separate control and data connections between the user and a server. You get in using a regular sign-in system. Essentially a password. Simple as that. Make sense?"

"Well, I guess I get it. It means they were dumb to do what they did."

"Not necessarily John. It's fairly easy to break into any web space once you know it's there and if you know how. So in a way hiding it on your machine was not such a bad idea. I mean, *John Smith*!"

I blushed, but that was that. We didn't bother to pursue it further. There was no need. That part of the story was done and we had to push on with the rest.

As soon as we hit town we headed for the local computer supplies and repair shop. All four of us tumbled over each other to get in. I put my machine on the counter. The salesman took one look at it and grimaced at the filthy battered object. "What can I do for you?"

He was a sack-like man, sagging in all directions. Not obese, but somehow spread out. He was bent to boot with an invisible weight pushing down on his shoulders. I took a deep breath. "I want you to connect this to the mains and boot it up."

"Why? What's wrong with it?"

"Nothing I hope. I just pray that there's a folder I want—need—on it."

Bentsag looked puzzled.

"The machine was stolen. It had my novels on it."

"My rate is £40 per hour. £40 minimum. Is that OK with you?"

"OK with me." I was starting to hop up and down. Not because I wanted to wee, but I just couldn't contain myself after all we had been through.

I watched with hawk eyes as he plugged the machine into the mains and connected up a mouse and a monitor. He switched it on. I heard the familiar sounds of it whirring and grinding into life. I couldn't see the monitor. Bentsag stared at it without emotion. I thought I was going to burst.

"Seems to be booting all right."

"Can I see the monitor, please?"

He swung it half round in my direction as the desktop display creaked into life. "The mouse too, please." He slid it across the counter and into my eager hands. I waited for the icons to come to life. They didn't. The screen was blue, displaying: Hard Drive Closed. Error. Login Required.

Bentsag stared at the screen. "So, what's the login code?"

I could barely speak. "I don't have it.

"Looks like you have a problem then."

"Anything you can do? I squeezed out"

"No, Sir. There's no way to open it without the login."

I turned to Susie with a pleading look and my heart in my boots.

She stepped forward. "Have you a workshop or back room I could use?"

"Sure, but it'll cost you."

Susie looked daggers.

"OK, OK." I jumped in. "Whatever. Not an issue."

Susie unplugged the monitor and the mouse and, pulling the mains plug from the wall, she picked up my PC and followed Bentsag to the back of the shop and into a small office. We followed. She put the machine down. "If I can run through some ideas on your laptop with an internet connection, John, it should only take me an hour to break in. I know this can be solved and I have some clues. The login will have something to do with Fer-de-lance."

"What can I do?"

"Nothing. You can't help me with this. I need to work alone. Pay him to shut the shop down for a couple of hours then go out, locking me in. Tell him to check on me after an hour."

I walked to the front of the shop and explained the position to Bentsag. 200 in cash had him eating out of my hand.

"Let's go for a stroll, boys."

The sun had come out but the streets were still shiny with rain. The buildings were brightly lit and glowed in the reflected sunshine. It cheered me up, but I still felt hollow. The failure to run my PC had brought me down. We strolled up to a park, picking up some coffees on the way.

"Drag, John."

"Yeh, drag, Biro. But if anyone can sort it out, it's Susie."

"You sure 'bout that?"

"Well, I live in hope."

"It springs eternal," added March.

"Semper Fi," added Biro.

We waited out the full hour and returned to the shop. I could see Susie and Bentsag with my computer at the counter. I took a deep breath then plunged in. Susie turned to us and smiled. She had done it!

"Is it OK?" My voice was raspy.

"Think so, John. As far as I can see all your files are there."

Biro, March and I faced the PC. It burst into life and I could see that all my icons were there. Totally freaked, I clicked on 'my documents'. The screen switched as my folders filled the screen. I scrolled through to 004 and clicked on it. It opened. I scanned it and wonder of wonders they were there. Both novels. I beamed round the room.

Taking my laptop out of my bag, I turned to Bentsag, "Could you drop this folder onto a couple of CDs while I copy it onto this?"

"Sure."

While he broke out a couple of discs and loaded one into my computer, I switched on my laptop and plugged in a link.

He burned the folder onto both discs while I copied the folder onto my laptop. He handed me the discs and we shut down both machines.

I paid off Bentsag and lumbered away to the SUV stuffing the discs into my inside pocket, zipping it up carefully and then tapping it twice to make sure they were secure.

I put the PC in the boot of the SUV and we gathered around. We waited for Susie to tell us the story.

"Ever since you showed me that equation, John, I've had numbers and symbols running through my head. I had a feeling we'd need a password or login to get into your machine. I guessed they would have locked it. Entry only with the right log in. I had some good ideas what that might be. I've been setting up codes and then breaking them in my head. Sometimes my math kind of runs on auto-pilot." She smiled at me then went on. "Once I was inside your PC I could follow the thread to the Fer-de-lance package. At this point there were two more walls, but my mind was racing. I'd got their code. The first wall was easy. The second was a lot tougher. I got there and I was in. I didn't open the

Fer-de-lance package, but I set up a neutral FTP function and winged the data back to the place it came from—somewhere in Russia. There are still traces on your machine, which I can't clear out quickly, John. So I suggest we dump the box in the deep, dark sea along with the guns."

"OK. I'm for that." I glanced at Biro and March. "Let's go first to the lockup and pick up the Merc, return this to the hire company and then take the boat out to sea."

March nodded his agreement. Biro was thinking. He turned to me. He gestured towards the Hispano, which had already gathered quite a crowd of stunned on-lookers. It was without doubt a most impressive car. "Could I put this in the lock-up for a few months until the dust settles?"

"Course you can. I'll lay out the wedge for a year's rental."

"You're a pal, John. 'Preciate it."

"No sweat, Biro. You've been a star. I couldn't have done this without you. Like I said we make a great team." I squeezed Susie's hand. I got her scent again. Meadow. I caught sight of us in reflection in the shop window. We did indeed look good together. She kissed me.

I walked over to the Merc, opened the boot and emptied out one of the weather bags. Biro lifted in the PC. He looked puzzled.

"It's dangerous for me to keep this, Biro. For anyone, come to that. It's no use to me now."

"Yeah, OK, John. Davey Jones beckons."

Biro called the lockup manager, then the boat hire company and set everything up. We drove down to the garages and I backed out the Merc. Biro inched the enormous limo in. It just fitted, but the doors wouldn't open and Biro had to clamber onto the back seats and then slide out through the boot. Very funny.

We returned the SUV to the hire company. They complained about its dirty, mud-spattered condition. I gave them an extra 200, which quickly shut them up.

The boat was ready to go when we arrived at the quayside. We climbed aboard and set sail. As we cruised away from the quayside I remembered my guru telling me about a letter written by his own master's predecessor sometime early in the last century.

It was something like this: "Your view that a soldier's career is inconsistent with the spiritual path is not sound. In his war Guru Jaimal had no hostile feeling towards the opposition. In the evening he would go among them and they respected him."

Chapter Thirty Seven

THE DEEP BLUE SEA

"God does not play dice."
Albert Einstein

Three miles offshore I watched Biro and March, bags in hand, walk to the stern. I nodded to Susie and we climbed up onto the bridge. We held the helmsman's attention while Biro and March disposed of the guns and the PC. Strangely he had BBC Radio 4 playing and there was an item on the economy. Some economist pundit was saying that growth figures were less than expected and what had been hoped for. Susie threw a V-sign at the radio and turned to me. She was flushed and angry.

"Wassamatter Susie?"

"It's that same old growth crap."

What d'you mean?"

"I mean the ludicrous and dangerous stupidity of capitalism is that it leads to the idea that economies and industries can grow and grow and grow. This is nonsense to anyone with half a brain. Growth can't just go on and on and on. If it did we would just grow ourselves right off the planet. On top of that resources are obviously finite. There's only so much we can take before the whole thing runs dry and we plough right into the ground. Whifflediff! End of story. Get it?"

"Yeah, I get it and my guess is that this has something to do with mathematics. Am I right?"

"You are and it does, John."

"Go on then, Susie. I know you're dying to tell me."

She laughed and once more touched my heart. Ain't love grand?

"There's a book called *Limits to Growth*, which examined the past thirty years of reality with the predictions made in 1972 and which found that changes in industrial production, food production and pollution are all in line with the book's position. These predictions were based on math principles and formulae. The scary thing is that the book predicted economic and societal collapse in the 21st century. Where we are right now."

She turned to the helmsman. "Have you a sheet of paper and a pencil I could use, please?"

"Sure." He opened a draw beside him and pulled out a notebook and a felt tip pen. "Here."

"Thanks." She leaned forward over a small worktop and started to write. I watched in a kind of enchanted way. She turned and handed the notebook to me. I looked at it intently:

$$y = \frac{\log\left(1 - (1-g) \times \frac{r}{c}\right) - 1}{\log(g)}$$

Susie watched over my shoulder. "This is the formula for calculating the amount of time left for a resource straining under the lash of constant growth."

"Doesn't mean diddlysquat to me, Susie."

"Didn't think it would, John. I just wanted you to see what just a few little symbols can do to explain big and very complicated things."

"OK."

"It's more than OK, John. It's awesome."

"I am starting to get it. Honest."

She gave the helmsman his notebook and pen.

"Can we head back to port now, please? I asked."

"Sure. You're the boss." He swung the wheel and the boat turned on its tail.

Biro looked at us and gave me a thumbs-up. So the deed was done. We went down onto the deck.

"Politicians sicken me. They're all liars and cheats."

"Copy that, Susie."

"Growth is a con. A smoke screen. They're having us on."

"Finite resources will not stretch to infinity," I conceded.

We joined Biro and March as they made their way up to the bows. The air was clear, the sky was blue and the spray flew off the bows. It was thrilling and beautiful. Susie took my hand. We were silent for a while just enjoying the freedom. Out of the blue Susie turned to me and asked, "D'you like classical music, John?"

"Course."

"Favourite three composers then?"

"Another music quiz?"

"Oh, c'mon, John. I just want to know."

I thought for a minute. Not easy to narrow it down. "Well, OK. Bach, Elgar, Palestrina."

"Wow. Bach and Palestrina go together. Very mathematical."

"Yes. Symmetric. I have always felt there was some kind of mathematical basis to Bach fugues and Palestrina's—what d'you call it—polyphonic compositions."

"Yes, polyphonic. But Fugues are only sort of polyphonic. They are really contrapuntal." She corrected me in her friendly way.

"That figures, Susie."

"But what about Elgar? That's a very different kind of music."

"Very English. Got that great feel like a John Constable painting."

"Constable's cloud paintings are a good example of the fractal principle too."

"How's that?"

"Comes back to that famous quote of Mandelbrot where he starts with clouds are not spheres."

"I think I might have heard that somewhere," I said, grinning.

Yes, well, there's a TV doc called *Clouds Are Not Spheres,* which you might have come across. I think it's been broadcast in the UK. It certainly has in the USA on PBS."

"Ah, yes. Maybe I have heard of it, Susie. Though I don't recall seeing the film."

"I think you would remember if you had, John. It's powerful stuff. Well, anyway, Constable captures the wrinkly, crinkly quality of clouds in a beautiful way."

"We should go to a gallery sometime to check them out."

"Yes, we should, John." She paused to look out over the rolling sea. "What's your favourite piece by Elgar?"

"Without doubt, *The Dream of Gerontius.*"

"I love that too."

It was amazing to have this love of *The Dream* in common with Susie. "To the glory of God, is how Elgar described that masterpiece."

"To the glory of God and The Regiment!"

"Yup."

"Cool." She kissed me lightly on the cheek and I returned the compliment.

The harbour was approaching fast. I walked over to Biro and shook him by the hand. "I'll never forget this, Biro. You did a real sterling job."

"Oh, you're too kind, John, my friend. I've had a great time and I am happy to be of service. Reminded me of the best days I spent with The Regiment."

Chapter Thirty Eight

EVENT HORIZON

The point of no return

We were lying side by side in bed. It had been a successful, fruitful day and we had all come out of it alive. Susie was reading to me from a scientific paper: "In general relativity, an event horizon is a boundary in space-time beyond which events cannot affect an outside observer. In layman's terms it is defined as the point of no return. That is the point at which the gravitational pull becomes so great that escape is impossible. The most common case of an event horizon is the one surrounding a black hole. Light emitted from beyond that horizon can never reach the observer. In the same way that any object approaching the horizon from the observer's side appears to slow down and never quite pass through the horizon, with its image becoming more and more *red-shifted* as time elapses. The travelling object, however, does not experience any strange effects and does, in fact, pass through the horizon in a finite amount of proper time.'"

She looked at me out of the corner of her eye then went on. "There's an interesting parallel here with chaos theory or what's now called complexity theory." Susie turned towards me. "Complex systems."

"Hang on, hang on. Complex systems . . . what d'you mean by that?"

"I mean living systems, John. Like us—you and me. Mammals, birds, fish, insects, microbes—all living things."

"OK. Press on."

"Yes?"

"Please, Susie."

"Complex systems have to find the balance between stability and order and the need to be able to change. So they tend to place themselves at what we call the edge of chaos. We see the edge of chaos as a place where there is room for innovation to keep systems vibrant and enough order to keep them from collapsing into mess. It really is a place of conflict and upheaval. It's tricky. If a system gets too close to the edge it will fall apart into incoherence, but at the same time if it drifts too far from the edge it will go rigid and dissolve. Complex systems can only flourish on the edge."

I laughed. "Sounds like us, Susie."

"The past few days!" She exhaled.

"Yes."

"The days of violence and glory."

"And fear, Susie."

"It didn't show."

"It was there."

We lay in silence for a few minutes until I found myself saying: "It sounds kind of like the boundary—the edge—of the Mandelbrot set."

"It does indeed, John. Yes. And boundaries are where interesting things happen."

"Do we have a boundary, Susie?"

"We are the boundary, John."

"Yes, but . . ."

"Thing is when complexity develops rapidly within a system there is a risk of it descending into chaos."

"Did we?"

"What, John?"

"Descend into chaos?"

"D'you think we did, Susie?"

"No, I don't think we did. We pulled it off perfectly, John."

"Really?"

"Yes, really . . . you did it."

"*We* did it, Susie."

"OK, we did it."

"Couldn't have done it without you."

"I would have thought Biro . . ."

"Ah, yes . . . well. Biro certainly saved the day, but you were the perfect support. In fact you *are* perfect, Susie."

"Oh, come on, John."

"All right. I'll put it like this, though, you are about as perfect as a human being gets."

"God! Give me a break."

"Is there a God?"

"Nice link, John."

"OK, but what d'you think? God or no God?"

"How would I know?"

"Well, you might have an opinion. Do you?"

"Yes, I do have an opinion, John."

"And . . . what is it?"

"What is what?"

"Your opinion, Susie. Don't be evasive."

"Watch it, son. Let's not fall out over God. Happens all too often."

"No, let's not do that. But what is your opinion?"

"Well, it seems to me that it is highly unlikely that complex forms like us, ants, snails and horses could appear randomly out of a warm, mud soup."

"I agree, Susie."

"Yeah." She lapsed into silence then moved to the side of the bed. She looked back at me over her shoulder with dreamy, faraway eyes. She got up, walked naked to the window and stood in the sunlight. I thought I was in heaven.

"So what d'you think's going on, John?"

I looked for the right words. "I guess evolution from a random series of events could produce physical forms, but I don't believe that science can explain consciousness. The issue seems to be avoided. Am I right?"

She picked up her gown from the chair beside her and slipped into it. She walked back towards the bed and sat on the corner.

"You're right. And to me self-consciousness is even more mysterious."

"Like the universe being aware of itself through us."

"Just so, John."

"I had a friend in my teens called Marcus, who used to quote from a philosopher called Schwaller de Lubicz. This guy said—if I remember correctly—the goal of the creation is the acquisition of consciousness or a reknowing of the thing in itself by itself."

"Makes sense, John."

"Marcus was at school with the god of science Richard Dawkins. He said he was a grim little dipstick even then."

"Never taken to him either. Evangelical atheists don't do it for me. Same as fundamentalist Christians and Muslims. Got their heads up their proverbial arses, I'd say."

I laughed. Susie had a good turn of phrase and she was open, which I had always thought was rare amongst scientists. "So how did you get interested in these things, John?"

"LSD, I guess."

"LSD!"

"LSD, yes. Lysergic Acid Diethylamide 25." I waited. She didn't say anything so I asked, "Ever tripped, Susie?"

"No. Should I have?"

"It wouldn't hurt."

"Tell me about it. What d'you get out of it?"

"My first LSD experience was terrifying because I made the stupid mistake of trying to hang on to my ego, my sense of I-ness and being John Smith. I refused to let go and blend into the experience. The acid was Uzbekistani and had been manufactured to the highest spec. It wasn't watered down. It was the real deal. Full strength and very pure. Even though I had that very bad experience first time, I recognised its power and potential. The second time I took it I had a guide known as Inside Mike. Inside had experimented with mescaline and peyote in the Mojave Desert. He helped me let go. He took me to a mirror and said: 'Look. You are the creator. You are everything. It is all you.' I let go into the experience. I stared into a crumpled up tissue for two hours, seeing whole universes being born and dying, listening to Bach's fugues—the music of the spheres." I paused, wondering if I had overstated my case.

Susie watched me. She didn't react for a minute.

I felt unnerved "Does that sound self-indulgent?"

She shook her head and smiled. "No. No, not at all."

"Oh, good." I felt relieved.

"So what did you conclude from it, John?"

I thought about this. "I believe like Aldous Huxley that LSD opens the doors of perception. My experience was awesome and it was shared by others. It was a new and eye-opening experience for me to see the world and the dancing atoms that we are. It put me in touch with the universe, with infinity. There's a famous recording of Bill Hicks doing a show when he talks about LSD. He said: on LSD I realized that all matter is merely energy condensed to a slow vibration, that we are all one consciousness experiencing itself subjectively. There's no such thing as death. Life is only a dream and we are in fact the imagination of ourselves." I paused again for effect. "It's the truth, Susie."

"I believe you, John. Physics and math say a lot about truth too, but nothing at all about beauty and moral judgements. I guess that whatever is particular about thought and mind lies right outside the scope of the physical sciences. Like you I see something very strange is happening in living matter."

"Yes. It surely is."

"I got a feeling, John, that these acid revelations have something to do with your guru. Am I right?"

"You are."

"So tell me, how it fits together?"

"Like this. Acid showed me that there was more to this life than met the eye—that we are infinite, universal mind, that we are consciousness itself and not just our physical bodies. I saw that matter—the physical, observable world is an illusion and that it's simply a projection of consciousness. I went East to study with my guru, to get to that consciousness without LSD to take me there."

I had said my piece. My cards were on the table. Susie was silent for a while. I waited for what was to come next out of the universal bag.

"But you know, John, apart from the mystery of consciousness it's even hard—impossible in fact—to explain how complex physical structures have emerged at all." She looked round at me.

I loved the way she talked as much as I liked what she was saying. "More, please."

"Well, take the bacterial flagellum."

"The what?"

"Bacterial flagellum."

"A flagellum is a motor. It's a thing like a tail, which sticks out from a bacterium and propels it. For example, a *sperm* cell uses its flagellum to propel itself through the female reproductive gear."

"So, what's so interesting about this bacterial flagel . . . ?"

"Flagellum."

"Flagellum."

"A bacterial flagellum is made of at least three parts—a paddle, a rotor, and a motor. It is very, very small—nano scale—and very, very complex—I'd say irreducibly complex."

"Why?"

"Gradual evolution of the flagellum faces massive hurdles. It's an incredible system, which is impossible to describe by a gradual step-by-step Darwinian process. The flagellum won't function until all the parts are in place. Like a mousetrap—without all five parts fitted together the trap is useless. So, where do all the parts come from and how do they know how to fit together if there is no plan in existence to tell them where to go?"

"Ah. Creation or evolution?"

"Just so, John, my dear."

"I've heard something like that argument too with regard to the eye. I mean, how could an eye evolve if it didn't know what it was evolving for if it didn't know that there was something to be seen?"

"You mean like half an eye is no use. There's nothing useful or directional between an eye and no eye at all."

"Yeah, that's what I mean. In the end we don't know. Maybe, maybe not."

"We'll just have to wait and see I guess, John."

"'Til we shuffle off this mortal coil . . . kick the bucket . . . wave off . . ."

"Yeah, well, it's the one thing we can be certain of, isn't it?"

"Death?"

"Yup."

"Way to go, John."

Chapter Thirty Nine

SAT CHIT ANAND

I am that

The thirty-ninth step.

That night I had the strangest dream ever. I was the guru! It was in fact a lucid dream. It started as a normal dream, but after a while I knew I was dreaming. Question is: what did it mean?

I had amazing recall and as soon as I woke I slipped out of bed, booted up my shiny new laptop and wrote down everything I could remember.

I was sitting on a raised platform giving some sort of a talk or presentation, in which I was saying something more or less like this: "What is a piece of rock made of? What is it that you touch? What is it *made* of? Atoms? And just what are they made of? The answer is mainly empty space, with tiny electrons, orbiting nuclei made of protons, and neutrons. These things, which are both vibrant energy, like light, and simultaneously particles are what we are made of—intangible, invisible fields of force bound together by a mathematical equation.

Real, solid things out there seem to become abstract concepts—seem to become the stuff of consciousness itself!

So what is real? In the end, it is all literally in the mind, for it is there that we *see*. We human beings see the world one way, insects see it another, and artists in yet other ways. A bee can see ultraviolet. Flowers look very different to them. A dragonfly sees with a compound eye, like lots of little eyes. Each of us has, it seems, our own universe, our own take on reality.

Sir Isaac Newton was a deep thinker. He was obsessively inquisitive and he was, above all, a spiritual man. His whole life was dedicated to avoiding the shadows and finding the substance. To get us going on the right track, to get us thinking right, Newton asked us to consider the following question:

Whence is it that nature does nothing in vain and whence arises all the order and beauty that we see in the world?

The more Newton thought about the order and the beauty he was a witness to in the world, the more he felt the presence of the creator in the universe. He helps us to see that Nature is not just dancing aimlessly in the dark. Wherever he looked he saw order and stunningly beautiful and complex beings. As he studied the order emerging from the apparent chaos around him, he was deeply moved and was left with a yearning to know the power that made him, this world, the planets and the stars.

Just like Newton, as we look around us at this world we too are often struck by its beauty and, at times, by its glory and its splendour. The whole show really is quite astonishing. It's awesome. It is exceedingly extraordinary when you stop, when you look, when you listen. Yes, the world is wonderful and marvellous to behold and to be a part of, and we can be moved by its sublimity, but let us never forget that it is nonetheless an illusion."

Wow! Where did all that come from?

When I had finished my presentation I opened the meeting to the floor and fielded questions from the audience. And here's a funny thing: *I* stood up and asked the first question. So here I was effectively talking to myself and in public and in a lucid dream! It was working on three levels and it reminded me of a piece I had read in the *Avatamsaka Sutra*, which we call the Flower Garland Sutra. It's about Indra's net, which was a vast network of precious gems hanging over the palace of the god Indra, so arranged that if you look at one jewel you see all the others reflected in it. It also says in that sutra that in every particle of dust there are present Buddhas without number. Wheels within wheels within wheels.

Now, back to my question. I asked the guru—me—if we had any free will or was everything determined. As the guru I thought about this for a moment or two then I laughed gently in an encouraging kind of way and said:

"When Isaac Newton came up with laws of motion and laws of gravity the picture that emerged was of a clockwork universe. It was of a machine that ticked on a predetermined course. All we needed to know was where it was now and what it was doing now and then we could predict the future forever. And there are two challenges to this. One is Quantum Mechanics, which says that in fact there is irreducible chance built into the very fabric of the universe. And you can't actually say exactly what it's doing now. You can't say exactly what it's doing ever. But the other is, things that come out of the Mandelbrot set and related parts of mathematics which say that even in a Newtonian world in practice you may not be able to predict the future. It can be deterministic in principle but not in practice.

This is how God created a system which gave us free will. It's the most brilliant manoeuvre in the universe: to create something, in which everything is free! How could you do that?"

I asked myself, "Are you asking me?"

"No, not really", I replied. "It's a rhetorical question." I paused and looked hard at myself.

As the guru I went on, "Albert Einstein refused to accept the idea of a dice-playing deity. He wrote a letter to Max Born in which he said, You believe in a God who plays dice and I in complete law and order. So he obviously felt that chance and deterministic laws were not compatible. And he preferred the deterministic laws. Now, what the Mandelbrot set and Chaos Theory and related things have done for us is to show that you can have both at the same time. So it's not whether God plays dice that matters, it's how God plays dice."

I have a belief that our individual consciousnesses can tap into the universal mind. In fact Carl Gustav Jung would have been surprised and delighted to know that the computer revolution, whose beginnings he just lived to see would give a new impetus to his theory of the collective unconscious: the idea that there is a well of consciousness, compounded of primordial, universal images that we all share—the sub-structure or background of awareness. Is this what I was doing—tapping into the collective unconscious, the universal mind? I wonder.

I took a few more questions and the meeting came to an end. I nodded to the two AK-toting heavies standing on either side of the stage. They glanced around the ground and the crowds. Then they led me out to a white stretch limo parked on the access road behind the tent where we'd been. I slid in. The car creamed away and we headed off. After a 10 minute drive we arrived at a helipad. There was a smart, stainless steel Jet Ranger (shades of the DeLorean DMC 12 but without the gull-wing doors!) sitting like an insect on the pad with its rotors slowly whirling. We clambered in. I strapped up and the rotors started to speed, burning and churning. Dust flew up around the Ranger as we lifted off and headed into the deep, dark red sunset. I sang.

"I'm building an ashram in St Tropez.

The girls come free, but the guys gotta pay.

I'm a guru

Wholly more holy than you . . ."

Chapter Forty

30,000 TANDAR EXIST

**Revealed in a cut-up of a
Conservative Party Pamphlet.
A technique prompted by the writing style of
William S Burroughs.**

We took turns driving to Edinburgh. I planned to return the Merc to the hire company at the airport and take a flight back to London. But before we did that I wanted to buy us all suits and have our photo taken in a proper studio. I asked Biro to book us into a good one for later that day.

We parked right outside John Lewis' Edinburgh branch on a double yellow line. To hell with it. As we'd learnt, rules are there to be broken. We scrambled out and went first to the menswear department. I wanted us all to have the same suits and the most expensive that they stocked. We had a fine old time parading around the store. We looked great. They were elegant suits by Hackett & Plim and cost nearly £700 a piece.

When we were satisfied with the fits I paid the bill and we kept them on for the photo shoot. Next stop ladies' fashion.

Of course it took Susie an age to find what she wanted, but we enjoyed watching her go through a series of outfits. She settled for a black Jaeger Bugle Bead Jacket at £500 and a black Jaeger Bugle Bead Pencil Skirt, which worked out at just over £300. I was stunned. She looked so powerful turned out like that.

I bought shoes, shirts and ties for us men. Susie chose a cream silk blouse and some beautiful black shoes with very pointed toes. We dressed and left the store, carrying our work clothes in J L bags.

Unsurprisingly when we got back at the car we found that we had picked up a parking ticket, which I had great pleasure tearing up and ceremoniously binning all the while singing Dylan's *Subterranean Homesick Blues*:

"Get jailed, jump bail, join the army if you failed.

Look out kid, you're going to get hit.

But users, cheaters, six-time losers hang around the theatres,

Girl by the whirlpool looking for a new fool:

Don't follow leaders, watch the parking meters."

We all chorused the final line as we sped off to the photographer's.

With the photos done and printed up we headed out to the airport, dropping March off at the rail station on the way. It was an emotional parting, but I felt we would be meeting again soon. For sure.

Biro booked us in business class on the next London flight as we skimmed through the Edinburgh evening traffic. We were in high spirits.

I handed the car back while Biro collected our flight tickets. I told them about the parking fine and laid an extra 200 on them to cover it. They seemed happy with this. And why not?

Chapter Forty One

SIG SAUER JIGSAW

"Once I lived the life of a millionaire . . ."
Jimmie Cox

All the pieces had fallen into place.

I hired a car at Heathrow and we headed into London. The sky was overcast and black, but the rain was holding off. Predictably the traffic was heavy and progress was slow. Susie sat next to me in the passenger seat and Biro was in the back.

"So how do you both feel about it now?"

"Feel about what?" Biro responded.

"Feel about what we've done."

"We got your novel back, didn't we John?" Susie looked hard at me. "Wasn't that the point?"

"Yeah, of course it was. But did we pay too high a price?"

They did not respond immediately. Then Biro eventually spoke again. "Price? What d'you mean, John?"

"I mean the guns, the violence . . ."

Biro guffawed. "That wasn't violence, John, at least not like the violence I've seen and been a part of."

"I guess not, Biro. But . . ."

Susie turned to me. "But what, John?"

"But we shot Gevorkian."

"I shot him, John."

"OK. You shot him, Biro, but I was there. I was a part of it. I must take my share of the responsibility."

"Fair enough, John. But we didn't kill him, did we?"

"No. We didn't kill him. But we might have wrecked his arm."

"Well, as I see it, that's just his tough shit. He took risks. He took liberties and now he's paying the price."

Susie put her hand on mine. "Don't beat yourself up, John. He's not a good man. Maybe it will teach him something."

It sure taught me something," I replied.

She squeezed my hand. "What did it teach you, John?"

"Taught me that the most valuable thing in this life is having friends. Good, trustworthy friends. That and a guru, of course." I laughed then looked over my shoulder at Biro. "You worried about Gevorkian coming after us?"

"What d'you mean, John? Revenge?"

"Yeah, Biro. Something like that."

He looked out of the car window at the leaden sky. "Never happen, John."

"Why not?"

"Two reasons. He knows we can take care of ourselves and that we'll stick together." He paused.

"And?" asked Susie.

"And Comb-over's on his case. For all he looks like a yard of sick hangin' out a hospital window, he's a pretty smart guy. He's well-established on the inside of the gang. He'll get 'em. I don't doubt it."

The traffic began to pick up speed as the rain began to fall. We were silent for a mile or so before I spoke again. "I've wondering, Susie, 'bout what you said about growth."

She didn't say anything so I went on. "I watched a talk on youtube recently by an American guy called Ray Kurzweil . . ."

"The singularity man."

"Yes, that's right."

Biro groaned. "Oh, here we go again. More science!"

Susie turned round to him. "No listen, Biro. This'll affect you . . . all of us."

"What will?"

"The growth of computing power. It's odd, but as computing power grows the machines actually shrink."

"Yeah, Susie. Even I knew that."

"Sorry, Biro, I didn't mean to be patronising, but the facts are astonishing."

"Go on then . . ."

"John?"

I thought for few seconds before I responded. "Well, as far as I recall, this guy Kurzweill said that when he was at College, which must've been about 40 years ago, the computer they used at MIT took up a whole building and now he had that much power in the cell phone in his pocket."

"That's right," said Susie, picking up the thread. "The technology is now a million times cheaper, a million times smaller and a thousand times more powerful."

"No shit!"

"No shit, Biro." Susie went on. "Fact is over time there's been a billionfold increase in computing capability per dollar."

"That is growth!" Biro was impressed.

I looked at him over my shoulder. "And, Biro, he talked of the sixth paradigm."

"The sixth paradigm . . . sounds like a sci-fi movie."

"Yeah, well, Biro, it may do, but it's sci-fact."

"Tell me more."

It was Susie's turn. "The sixth paradigm is computing at the nano scale. They describe it as three dimensional self-organising molecular circuits."

"And that means?"

"And that means, Biro, a computer of enormous power in nothing bigger than a blood cell. Can you imagine?"

"No, I can't, Susie."

We all laughed this time. All the pieces fitted.

When I finally made it back to my house I needed reassurance and calm so I pulled out my copy of the Chandogya Upanishad and read:

'There is a Spirit which is mind and life, light and truth and vast spaces. He contains all works and desires and all perfumes and all tastes. He infolds the whole universe and in silence is loving to all. This is the Spirit that is in my heart, smaller than a grain of rice, or a grain of barley or a grain of mustard seed, or a grain of canary seed, or the kernel of a grain of canary seed. This is the Spirit that is in my heart, greater than the earth, greater than the sky, greater than heaven itself, greater than all these worlds. This is the Spirit that is in my heart. This is Brahman.'

This more or less confirmed my guru's opinion which, you'll hopefully recall, I quoted at the beginning of this book.

Unbelievably I was still unable to decide what to do with the money I had left over. I knew I must give it back. I opened the floorboard and took out the rest of the cash. I loaded it all into the briefcase and left the house. I walked two blocks until I came to the street of the burned down house. Surprisingly the skip was still there. Nothing had changed. Nothing had moved. I knew then what I had to do. Fate had decided this for me. I checked up and down the street and, seeing no one, I pushed the case deep down the side of the skip and out of sight. I sauntered back up the street feeling a lot lighter and, of course, a lot poorer, singing contentedly to myself:

"Once I lived the life of a millionaire
Spending my money, I didn't care.
I carried my friends out for a good time
Buying bootleg liquor, champagne and wine.
Then I began to fall so low
I didn't have a friend, and no place to go.
So if I ever get my hand on a dollar again
I'm gonna hold on to it till them eagles' green.
Nobody knows you when you're down and out."

Chapter Forty Two

THE LAST STRAW

'Solve et Coagulum'
He separates in order to unite
Swiss Alchemist and Philosopher, Theophrastus
Paracelsus Bombastus Von Hohenheim

I slept well that night. My heart was light with Susie curled around me but I did have a dream. And, guess what? My guru again.

"You are it, John. You are the thing in itself. Nothing and everywhere. Like a fractal you go in and in and in, repeating the same pattern over many scales. The universe is knowing itself through us—through our consciousness. The alchemist Paracelsus said 'He separates in order to unite'. So we are the universe becoming aware of itself.

"Fuck me," I responded. "Whoops, sorry."

"No problem, John. 'Fuck' is just a sound. There's nothing wrong with the word. Could be 'cufk' or 'ufck'. There is no such thing as 'bad' language either, John. There is just language—neither good nor bad. The label 'bad' is a human construct and it's meaningless. 'Fuck' somehow works best, don't you agree?"

"Sure do, boss."

"I am not your boss, John. You are your own boss. You are the universe. You are nothing and everywhere, remember?"

"Yup, I recall. Years ago."

"You're a good boy, John. You have learnt your lesson. You have done well. Never forget the wise words of your other mentor, John: 'Don't follow leaders, watch the parking meters.'"

That line again. I had to laugh as he drifted away and out of sight. I loved him and he loved me.

Chapter Forty Three

"The laws of nature and the initial conditions
are such as to make the universe as interesting as
possible. As a result, life is possible but not too
easy. Always when things are dull, something turns
up to challenge us and to stop us from settling into
a rut. Examples of things which make life difficult
are all around us: comet impacts, ice ages, weapons,
plagues, nuclear fission, computers, sex, sin and
death. Not all challenges can be overcome, and so
we have tragedy. Maximum diversity often leads to
maximum stress. In the end we survive but only by
the skin of our teeth!"
Freeman Dyson, Physicist

We never went back to our respective homes. We sent in a removal
team to empty both my house and Susie's flat then to deliver
everything to us in Cambridge. We settled in easily. It was late

summer and there was a hint of autumn in the air. We could see the river through the weeping willows from our balcony.

Biro and March were the witnesses at our quiet wedding a month later at Stoke Newington Town Hall. Oscar was my best man. I knew that this deal was for life whatever came our way.

As we were leaving the Registry Office at the end of the ceremony a beautiful uniformed police constable called Isabelle arrived with a gift from Comb-over: a pretty little Jack Russell puppy. We called her Jane.

We had a great party later that night at the Hiawatha Club in Soho. I promised Susie then I would tell her about my guru on our honeymoon in the Highlands, which was precisely what I did.

March never did write about our adventures. He left that to me. His book on the 9/11 tragedy/fiasco was published to great acclaim in the same year.

Susie had recently made a new friend, a literary agent, called Margaret Freeman. She helped to publish March and she liked my writing. It was ironic though. She preferred my first novel *Clusterfuck* and very quickly found a publisher for it. Set in '68, it was the story of a renegade, pot-smoking platoon of grunts cut off behind Vietcong lines. After much mayhem they eventually manage to break out by sea.

The book went down very well and to rave reviews. So much so that within three months Margaret had sold the film rights to a Hollywood studio. Two months after that the film was in pre-production and, believe it or not, they didn't change the basic storyline even though six different writers were employed to work on the dialogue. They altered the title to *Green as Grass*, punning on the pot smoking and to make it more palatable to their American audience. This was all fine by me as I looked at my swollen bank account. I was happy with the final, approved version they were going with. Like I've observed before, there is a God.

You may think that is a bit of a cheesy ending to the story but, let me tell you, as Bachman-Turner Overdrive put in a song: You ain't seen nothin' yet!

You may also think I'm cheating here, dear reader but I'm going let Peter Høeg have the last word in this story. In the final paragraph of his novel *Miss Smilla's Feeling* for Snow he wrote:

> *"Tell us, they'll come and say to me. So we may understand and close the case. They're wrong. It's only what you do not understand that you can come to a conclusion about. There will be no conclusion."*

I rest my case. May good fortune pursue you relentlessly just as it did me and just as it continues to do and may love and all that goes with it be yours . . .

Reviews

You've heard of books you can't put down, well I couldn't close this book. Compulsive reading, thoroughly enjoyable. David Russell Smith. Film Producer.

Nigel Lesmoir-Gordon is a very funny writer. Kathy Harty. Producer at HBO.

Nothing is as it seems and nothing is subject to the usual laws of reality in this book, peppered by snippets of advanced mathematics, deep spiritual truth and cosmic science, as well as a whole belly-full of hilarious action and real laughter. Alastair McNeilage. Author.

Nothing and Everywhere is thoroughly entertaining—humorous and tough by turns. Will Shutes. Writer and Art Historian.
I found this story gripping and very readable. Piers Jessop. Film Director.

Exquisite, enlightening prose! Pasquale Falbo. US National Guard Fighter Pilot.

There are so many pearls of wisdom contained in this book. I am going to have to read it again. Jimmy Audrey. Author.

I really enjoyed this book. It's quirky and it captured my attention. Samantha Mills. Yoga Teacher.

Pacy and entertaining. It's very engaging and leaves me wondering what will happen next.
William Rood. Author and artist.

It's strong on dialogue with a sense of screenplay as befits a film-maker. Mike Pitman. Author.

Nothing and Everywhere is certainly an original work and I can well see it being picked out and celebrated as such. Damien Enright. Author.

Lightning Source UK Ltd.
Milton Keynes UK
UKOW050815011211

182962UK00001B/151/P